The Silent Crossing

THE
SEAGULL
LIBRARY OF
FRENCH
LITERATURE

The Silent Crossing

PASCAL QUIGNARD

TRANSLATED BY CHRIS TURNER

LONDON NEW YORK CALCUTTA

Seagull Books, 2024

Originally published in French as Pascal Quignard, *La barque silencieuse. Dernier Royaume VI*
© Editions du Seuil, 2009

First published in English by Seagull Books, 2013
English translation © Chris Turner, 2013

ISBN 978 1 8030 9 361 1

British Library Cataloguing-in-Publication Data
A catalogue record for this book is available
from the British Library

Typeset and designed by Seagull Books, Calcutta, India
Printed and bound by WordsWorth India, New Delhi, India

CONTENTS

TRANSLATOR'S ACKNOWLEDGEMENT

I would like to thank Professor Leslie Hill of the University of Warwick and my fellow translator Marie-Dominique Maison for a number of very helpful suggestions in relation to this translation.

CHAPTER 1

I shall have spent my life seeking out words that I
lacked. What is a literary man? Someone for whom
words falter, jump about, elude his grasp, lose their
meaning. They are always trembling slightly beneath
the strange form they end up inhabiting nonetheless.
They neither speak nor hide anything: they signal
relentlessly. One day when I was looking in the Bloch
and Wartburg dictionary for the origin of the word
corbillard (hearse), I found there a horse-drawn boat
transporting unweaned infants. The next day I went
to the National Library, which at the time was in the
rue de Richelieu in Paris' second arrondissement,
housed in the old palace formerly occupied by
Cardinal Mazarin. I consulted a history of ports. I
noted down three dates: 1595, 1679 and 1690. In
1595, the so-called *corbeillats* arrived in Paris on

Tuesdays and Fridays. The bargemen first unloaded the freight, then took off the tightly swaddled infants, fastened upright in their little boxes on the deck. They set them down on top of barrels on the river-bank; the little shackled babies were then restored to their mothers one by one by a man known as the *meneur de nourrissons* (literally, the leader of unweaned infants). The next day at dawn—that is to say, every Wednesday and Saturday—the *corbeillats* transported other little ones from Paris to Corbeil, so that they could suck the teats and drink the milk of nurses in the countryside and forests. In 1679 Richelet wrote the word as *corbeillard*. °In 1690 Furetière spelt it *corbillard* and defined it as a horse-drawn boat that goes to Corbeil, a little town seven leagues from Paris. So, in the days when Malherbe, Racine, Esprit, La Rochefoucauld, La Fayette, La Bruyère, Sainte-Colombe and Saint-Simon were living in Paris, the *corbillard*, which now means 'hearse', was a boat filled with babies floating beside the banks of the Seine and howling.

CHAPTER 2

Louise Brulé

On 20 May 1766 Louise Brulé, being afflicted with an illness that caused her to fear she may die, resolved to bring home her one-year-old infant whom she had put out to nurse at Montargis. A *meneur de nourrissons* by the name of Louis brought the baby in a *corbillard* from Montargis to the Port Saint-Paul. Upon arrival, the child was found to be dead. The watch informed Louise Brulé. The clerk of the Briare horse-drawn boat company, awaiting the infant's arrival, placed the body on a barrel lid. The witness statement made on 8 June 1766 ran as follows:

> An unknown woman came to the guard house. In tears, she told us that she came to see her child. After telling her that he was dead, we required her to tell us her name. Said she was called Louise Brulé, wife of

Damideaux, he being a domestic servant in the house of Jannier, a peasant farmer living in the rue de Sentier, she living in the rue de Cléry. Said that on 25 February 1765 she had entrusted her male child to a nurse with a layette appropriate to his state. Said it was the case that she had learnt by letter from the nurse ten months ago that the child was ill, whereas the nurse had previously told her that he was well and that he needed a gown, which she provided. Said she asked to see him and received a reply from the nurse's husband that the child was barely able to withstand the journey. Said she offered to pay for his illness. Said that since this time she had had two letters from the husband saying that the child was well one week and ill the next, that he had a slow fever and that it was the effect of the teeth coming up into his lips. Said she received no other news at all and, out of maternal affection and wishing to see him, they sent their cousin with two letters, one to the parish priest, one to the nurse's husband. Said she no longer remembers the content of the letters, since it was her husband who wrote them and she, not being able to read, did not read them. Said she felt ill and close to death and wanted to see him again. Said that, her cousin having left, she was greatly astonished to see him again today telling her that her child had died on the journey. Said that she cannot recognize him in his present state since she saw him only on the day that she brought him into the world. Said that she recognizes the cloth from which his layette is made. Said that she does not know where her husband is, that she believes him to be in the country with his masters because of the fine weather.

On 10 June 1766, her husband not having returned, Louise Brulé was found unconscious on the quayside. She was taken home on 11 June. On 17 June she was found dead in her bed by her husband Damideaux who had returned from the small town of Sèvres.

The witness statement of 8 June 1766 may be summarized tragically: a sick mother, at the moment the unknown of death is about to engulf her, wishes to see her only child again and does not recognize him.

The child is *the unknown of birth*. The text of Louise Brulé's statement is clear: 'Said that she cannot recognize him in his present state since she saw him only on the day that she brought him into the world.' This remark by Louise Brulé goes to the heart of everyone's origins. Whoever he may be, whatever the century and whatever the nation, every child is at first an unknown. Every human destiny is the unknown of bringing-into-the-world, entrusted to the unknown of death. I am currently copying out the archives Arlette Farge entrusted to me in the days when we ate dab and whelks in garlic together in the rue de Buci. What Louise Brulé called *meneur de nourrissons* I have decided to call destiny.

CHAPTER 3

Quai de la fausse rivière

The house where I write looks out on to the dead arm of a river. To the east of the garden, on the dead arm of the Yonne, sheltered from barges and the little sailing boats, is the kingdom of the ducks, the swans, the willows, the black boats. Beyond a little stone stairway that goes down to the landing stage, where the boats full of rainwater are tied up and where the white slugs crawl along and the frogs jump, the bank that extends towards the north becomes a wharf called the Quai de la fausse rivière. °In the past the horse-drawn *gabarres* followed the towpath. The roof and the landing stage of the tally office jutted out to the west of the île de Sens.

A spade, a pair of pruning shears and an axe for the kindling, two rubber boots for the spongy ground and a yellow umbrella for the sky, a pencil and the back of envelopes—the solitary life is not vastly expensive when compared with the seven happinesses that go with it.

It's just days.

No other music in this world than the sound of the water and the cautious boats of the anglers, who gently slide down their anchors before casting their lines in the mist that hovers over the grey water.

CHAPTER 4

In times past, Maria Mallarmé and her little brother got into their father's boat at Sens and went down the Yonne. They fished for pike opposite the island.

°In those days Stéphane was still called Étienne.

Once upon a time the child Étienne Mallarmé floated happily along here.

CHAPTER 5

Laodamia

It happened that the dead Protesilaus was granted permission to return to earth and spend a day with his wife.

Yet he hesitated.

He loved Laodamia. That is what Ovid says.

Laevius says that Protesilaus so loved life that he was reluctant to live again for only a single day.

Catullus says he feared the emotion that would grip him when he reached out his hands towards Laodamia. He had the impression that his body would not be able to desire again; that once his sex had swelled, it would no longer be able to slip into her; that once he had penetrated her, he would no longer be able to remain erect deep within her; that he would be incapable of giving his wife the delight she had known for such a short span in his arms.

For Protesilaus had known Laodamia only a single day. On the morrow of his marriage he was already aboard the Greek vessels sailing towards Troy.

In the end, Protesilaus accepted the offer the gods made to him. He left Hades and came back up to Earth. He was reunited with Laodamia. Laodamia threw open her arms. Protesilaus grasped them. The night was short. Protesilaus' potency returned for a moment. It found satisfaction in the darkness. When the night ended, the shades took him back among the shades.

After his departure, Laodamia killled herself: she had slept with Protesilaus twice. Once before he left. Once more before he left again.

She had known only farewells from the man.

Laevius gave his tragedy a strange title, the very penning of which is already an embrace: *Protesilaodamia*. Catullus loved this legend. Ovid quoted it repeatedly.

*

Who has experienced anything other than Protesilaus? Who has felt anything other than Laodamia? The single day. The single night.

*

It seems to the body, as it falls asleep, that, before it plunges into sleep, it disconnects.

The human body in the darkness is like a boat slipping its moorings, leaving the earth, drifting.

CHAPTER 6

Salomon of London

Joseph Haydn was at work in his little house at 21 Seilerstätte. It was ten o'clock at night. He was composing the *Nocturnes for the King of Naples*. Suddenly he saw a stranger, who came into his room, doffed his hat and said, 'I am Salomon of London. I have come to fetch you. Have your luggage ready tomorrow morning.'

Joseph Haydn took ship for London, where he suddenly found fame.

CHAPTER 7

The City from the Other World

The port was grey and deserted.

On 1 November 1628, King Louis XIII rode into a totally silent, dead town filled with corpses.

Only the Atlantic was still there, rolling forward its white waves.

La Rochelle had become a city from Another World.

As they fell, a few ghosts still had upon their lips the shape of the cries they had uttered.

The white gulls flying above gobbled up their flesh in strips.

*

Men are shipwrecked souls from another world, with previous lives behind them, approaching a shore.

*

There are no children. There are only little, dwarfish, wrinkled, bald, toothless, dripping-wet heads. Tiny blood-spattered old people who emerge from a mother's vagina.

There are only ancestors' faces, as there are only ancestors' names.

*

At Antwerp in 1421, at the gate to the cemetery, the Dominican fathers built a labyrinth. They painted its walls with flame-coloured paint, from the vaults to the flagstones. The light illuminating this suite of enigmatic cells came from nine skylights with red stained-glass windows, in order thoroughly to convey the idea of a blazing furnace. In those windows one glimpsed, chained together amid the flames, an infinity of figures of scrawny naked men and scrawny naked women uttering cries that remained unheard.

*

I left Le Havre in 1958. I remember there was a gusty wind. The sky was white. The sun was low in the sky, round and white, so wan. It was the beginning of winter. I paid a visit to the Boys' Grammar School chapel. The civil-engineering firm that was rebuilding the ruins of the school had knocked the chapel down a few days before. I had been an altar server there for three years. I walked with my head lowered. I always walked head down. I so liked to charge forward with my head down. Head down with embarrassment and shame. Head down with reading and fear. Head down with silence and sin. Head down, particularly, to make headway against the unimaginable, almost animalistic violence of the wind. I went through the Saint Roch graveyard. I charged towards the windy city. Oh city, which had not entirely grown back yet amid the dust of the stones. City whose new walls—°all the little Perret buildings—were trying to rise as white as the sky where the winter's snows were gathering. I had put all the money I had to my name in the pocket of my flannel shorts. I threw the little coins into the rubble. I threw the money into the ruins of the place where I had taken the collection, at daybreak, holding out an aluminium plate. °One day, a hunter from the reindeer-hunting days—it was the day he abandoned the Grotte Carriot—left behind him two little seashells in a cleft at the base of an engraving he had made on the cave wall with a flint.

The ruins of a Christian chapel in the drizzle, in the sticky seaside cold, to the right of the covered area of the playground of the Boys' Grammar School where my fellow pupils pushed me, caressed me, in the foul stench of the three wooden sheds—standing side by side—of the toilets. °I can still see the insubstantial, white coins slipping between the strips of plaster in 1958, just after the *coup d'état*.

CHAPTER 8

The Dust Devil

'Dust devil' is the name given to a tiny little tornado, tall as two or three men standing on one another's shoulders, which whips up dust or straw in the month of August. The devil comes in the stormy season, a yellow column that meanders as it advances. It is a luminous, grainy form, preceding thunder and heralding lightning. It whirls round at great speed above the furrows, whipping up earth, or along a riverbank, snatching up the sand, or along the path, picking up bits of straw and thistledown, and it collapses most often in the branches of a wood.

Or it crashes on the surface of water.

It sometimes happens that the night doesn't entirely withdraw from the days of our lives. Our bodies then have reactions in the daytime that are not in keeping with the hour. They still bear the countenance of the past night. Even at noon we are still experiencing a nightmare. Even when we put our key in the door at the end of the working day, we are still upset by those we saw again in our dreams and, particularly, by what they said to us. It's no use rubbing our eyes. It's no use splashing water on our cheeks and brows. The night leaves a number of lingering images that glow with a light that is certainly not that of the starlit day.

Dream images have about them something of pebbles in water. Pebbles that sparkle beneath the freezing current, as it glides between the clumps of mint. Their beauty begs us bend down. We cannot resist the urge to kneel in the marvellous fragrance that rises from the little downy, serrated leaves of the mint plants that we crush on the banks of the Yonne. You roll your sleeves up above your elbows. You plunge in your hand and its flesh begins to shiver with cold.

Your freezing, white fingers gather up these stones from the transparent depths and bring them back into the light. The water drips from them; the air darkens them; one's eyes become despondent—I am speaking of the most richly textured moments of our lives. Their attraction fades; we no longer know what these once-shimmering stones were trying to tell us; we no longer know why, spontaneously, we went down on our knees.

They were fearsome eyes. They were silk dresses and stunning bosoms. They were the sex organs of both sexes; torn-up musical scores; provincial furniture; a president yellow as wax; a pointed nose; two friends.

Dull pebbles. Dull pebbles.

*

The little two-sided haematites, which the women of antiquity wore in Egypt and at Athens, Rome and Constantinople until the day they gave birth, are called uterine amulets. The pregnant woman was carved on the front. She was seated in her work chair with its two rams' heads. Between her thighs her womb was represented in the form of a cupping glass locked with a key. The parturient carried a club in her hand. On the back of the amulet the name Ororiouth was written in Greek characters. The Greek word *haematite* literally meant 'blood stone'. When plunged into water, the little oblong stone became as red as flowing blood again.

*

This is precisely what the past is: everything that passes through the door that leads down into the shadows.

Horus alone turns the key of birth or awakening.

It isn't memory but dreams that are the biological mirror in which the dead are reflected.

The Greeks gave the name 'demon' to this overseer—deep within us—of the reliquary.

The child Harpocrates, standing at the mothers' door, with a finger on his lips and the key of birth in his other hand, leaves closed the round sac that sucks in the father's sperm and must contain it for ten lunar months. He protects the ceaseless metamorphoses of the fetishes. A kind of god with a silencing finger similarly oversees the cephalic cave. He amends the memories we retain of the deceased by our excessive appeals to their absence. For we embellish their speech through the silence maintained by the virtually divine simulacra that arise out of their deaths. No one among the living now contradicts what we invent. They are pictures and compositions that become increasingly symmetrical, whose narrator is increasingly legendary—has become an ass, an octopus, a phallic bird, a butterfly or moth, water mint or a thistle—whose content is increasingly a thing of wonder. Thrilling scenes in which a single painter reigns. That painter is simply an image that will always be lacking from the depths of the body. A little penis paintbrush, predating even the protective red gemstone, for it is because our species is sexed that we carve two-sided stones, make diptyches, form parallels, construct dialogues. Oppositions, the unending source of the inventions made by the signs of language, are detached once and for all, as they take shape and bed down within us, from the power of their models. They stand further and further off from the chaos they destroy as they bring order to it.

They are great figures of mourning in which we muffle the cries.

We leave out the coarseness of bodies.

We wipe out the truth.

We love these figures at last, when we have entirely redrawn and forgotten them.

Then we keep our own finger pressed against our closed lips, so that no one reminds us of our lie.

CHAPTER 9

On 24 August 410 the Gothic army entered Rome. It was sacked in two days. The third night it was burnt. Rome's Christians gathered and bewailed the fact that the tombs of the apostles had been of no assistance to them. At that point, Augustine conceived *The City of God*, in order to set an image of an indestructible, eternal city against the memory of the ruined, blackened, smoking imperial City. Two capitals would henceforth share the world between them. A visible, museum-like, broken, pillaged, burnt, nostalgic, senescent capital and an invisible, dreamable, eternally new capital, a capital of treasures and promise, that would rise up on the Day of Judgement. Augustine initially planned to call the book he had conceived *The Two Cities*. That title came to mind because Tichonius had written: 'There are two kingdoms and two kings,

Christ and the Devil. The one desires the world, the other flees it. The one has Jerusalem as capital, the other Babylon.' But, in the end, Augustine changed the title on the grounds that only the better of the cities should be named, since that was the one called to have sole empire over the world. Books I to III were published in 413. Books IV and V in 415. Volume VI followed in 417.

I moved Augustine's two kingdoms back a notch in time. Before birth, after birth—these were the two gateways. A unique experience, with its metamorphosis standing out against a backcloth of death. A death I stubbornly refused to constitute as an ontological world. There were not three kingdoms, then. Only two kingdoms, like those two cities at the dawn of the Middle Ages, would wander in space, the one being the end of the other, ghosting the earth into a world. In Augustine the city of God *wanders about* the world. The world is a mixed entity: the century and eternity, the past and times of yore, the fruit and the sap. So far as I was concerned, I did not seek a God in the secular world any more than I saw a world in death. I was simply looking on the surface of the earth for the memory of She who returned my gaze. She whose flickering eyes melted an other with bliss. The shadow of the distant one, the shadow of the shadow, for a shadow, far—very far—behind each body, originating before it, is cast over the whole life of each human being. For, whatever Paul says, it is not death that casts this shadow over the world. It is the Lost One, who goes from our lives in the light of the first day, who projects that shadow endlessly. This shadow cast in time, from very far back in time, is called melancholy. Starting out from that melancholy, everything assumes a marvellous countenance.

Nudus exii de utero matris. I came naked from my mother's womb. Naked, I shall return to the earth. For, bringing nothing to this world, we shall take nothing with us beyond the black portals.

*

Exii. I have gone out. This is exile.

Once exposed to the sun's rays, the red gem immediately darkens.

The relationship we have from birth with abandonment and the lost, with water, absence, need, shadow and solitude is merely revived on the occasion of the deaths with which the course of our lives is studded. Abandonment is at the back of our minds. We are orphans of a joy which, when it welled up within us shortly after we emerged into the sunshine of this earth, had as yet no memory before it in which to be recalled.

o'What is hell?' asked Massillon. The absence of Last Judgement. What does the absence of Last Judgement mean? Impenitence. 'Here,' he exclaimed, 'are the most terrible words of the Scriptures. They are at John 8:21, when God exclaims *Ego vado, et quaeritis me, et in peccato vestro moriemini*. I go my way, and ye shall seek me, and shall die in your sins. This is the promise of the Gospels: abandonment by God, the death of God, ultimate impenitence. What is abandonment by God in the century? Loneliness. What is ultimate impenitence in time? Hell.'

CHAPTER 11

The pains he experienced were so intense that from time to time he lost his sense of discernment. °These are the words Cardinal Mazarin used to reply to the Queen Mother who questioned him about his condition. It was, strictly speaking, impenitence that was advancing in Mazarin's soul. °He himself told Lionne on 1 November 1659:

'I am so weary that I cannot go on.'

Brienne wrote: 'On the eve of Louis XIV's marriage with the Spanish Infanta, which was 18 June 1660, the Queen Mother, having come to visit him in his chamber, asked the first minister of the kingdom how he fared.'

'Ill.'

Then, without adding another word, he threw back his blanket, slowly brought out his leg and pulled his bare thigh out of the bed. Brienne says it was like Lazarus emerging from the grave. His leg and thigh were so emaciated, livid and covered in white blotches ringed with red swellings that the queen could not keep herself from crying out. From that day on, the cardinal lived prostrate on a mattress—even in his coach, to which he was carried by the four corners of his mattress, and where he was placed on another mattress of leather and wool. On 6 February 1661 it was very cold. It happened that the bedchambers caught fire. Brienne rushed to his master. He found the captain of the guard carrying the cardinal on his back. Mazarin was shrieking with fear. Brienne says you might have taken him for Anchises on Aeneas' back fleeing flaming Troy. They managed to lay him down. He was still quaking with the fear he had felt when confronted with the burning panelling. 'Death seemed painted in his eyes,' writes Brienne. To distract him, when his suffering had left him near the end of his tether, they carried him round his palace in the rue de Richelieu on a mattress folded in the bottom of a sedan chair. He sent for twelve doctors to examine him and find a way to reduce his pain. In the end, he turned to Guénaud and said:

'Guénaud, how long have I left to live?'

'Two months,' replied the doctor.

'I am grateful to you for your frankness, Guénaud, as much as a friend can be.'

And he immediately began to detest Guénaud. From that day onward, Cardinal Jules Mazarin cast off fear and plunged into terror. 'Guénaud said so, Guénaud said so,' the cardinal kept on repeating, his eyes gleaming with involuntary tears. The day after the doctors were consulted, Louis de Brienne spotted the cardinal in his sedan chair, being carried from room to room and into his gallery to admire his paintings. The cardinal saw the young man and called to him: 'Come forward, Brienne. Don't hide behind the doors. I'm just a dead man, presenting no other danger to those who mix with him than his horror.'

There were two guards in front of them carrying torches.

Weeping, the cardinal said to Brienne:

'Look at this fine Correggio. Look at this sombre Rembrandt. Look at this Venus painted by Titian. Look at this Flood by Antonio Carracci. Of all I have loved it is the finest. Ah, my friend Guénaud said so.

See, my friend, it hadn't occurred to me that, to reach the other world, it was necessary to abandon judgement—that is to say, beauty—at the same time as life.'

Heracles, Admetus, Dionysos, Orpheus, Tiresias and Achilles all descended into the Underworld and came back. On their return, they told of what they had seen. They related, as best they could in words, the deeply moving faces they had encountered, the old black light, all the old affection. Jesus descended into Hell like the other heroes. But we know nothing of Jesus' Hell. He is the only hero who did not have the strength or courage to recount to the living his visit to the dead.

Ariston also pointed out to the Greeks that, 'When Ulysses had descended among those who breathed no longer, conversing with numerous famous shades, he did not wish to see their queen.'

Why did Ulysses not wish to see the Queen of the Night?

Why did Ulysses the Sailor feel hatred for the woman who fired the knight Lancelot with such passion?

Why did Jesus not wish to say anything of what he had seen among the dead?

Then Dante took the path of Owein, Tungdal, Drythelm, Aeneas, Ulysses and Gilgamesh and descended in his turn.

CHAPTER 13

For a week it was feared that death would claim Madame de La Fayette. When Madame de Sévigné was informed, she retorted that her illness would at last have a name. Madame de La Fayette died on 26 May 1693. °Madame de Sévigné took up her pen again and, on 3 June 1693, wrote: 'She was mortally sad.'

*

When you slip your hand into the sea for an instant, you touch all shores at a stroke. It is the same with slipping one's foot into death, by which one leaves time.

*

I am looking at an old seventeenth-century drawing in a red tortoiseshell frame. The island is near. The boat is coming in. A naked man is leaning on the pole. He is about to bring the boat to shore.

The strand is full of shades. This is Hell. Tall trees overhang the damned, and steep rocks too, coming to a halt above faces open-mouthed and weeping. In the branches of the trees, at the very top, there are sudden shafts of light done in white chalk, dazzling rays of sunlight. They whiten the old blue paper, which has turned grey. They come from the world of the living. I grasp the frame—*le cadre*—though they didn't use that word at the time, but said *corniche*—cornice. I grasp the old tortoiseshell cornice. I turn it over. There is a label stuck on it, written in an old, dry, dull violet ink that is almost brown with age: 'Study for the Banks of the Acheron, Geoffroy Meaume'.

CHAPTER 14

The Last Tourney

He loved to go about on all fours. That was his passion. He loved to howl in the kennels. They say he fought the pugs and mastiffs 'mouth to mouth' for their bones. And when he managed to get the best morsel from them, in his delight at having prevailed he returned to give it back to them 'teeth to fangs'. His mother had been barren for six years, to the point that her husband became annoyed. One evening, at the foot of her bed, after first kneeling down, she told God, throwing her arms out in front of her, that since her husband hated her, she was ready to be impregnated by any creature from the other world. So saying, she pulled up her chemise. It was in this way that she conceived the son she called Gowther, because he cried night and day. He was the father of William the Conqueror. As soon as he was born, friends and family nicknamed him the

Devil. He did not suck at the breast but stuck out his mouth and tore into his nurses' breasts. When he reached the sixth wet nurse, the women who had charge of him asked a craftsman to make a hole in a cow's horn, to protect their teats as the baby extracted the milk. He never learnt his letters. He tore out his playmates' eyes with his fingers and munched them. If he saw a priest or a nun, he rushed at them with a club and hit them, leaving them for dead, though not before he had lifted their clothing and left his seed in the orifices thereby exposed. He had countless children by women who had sworn vows of virginity. So great was the terror he spread about the provinces that his father the king banished him. The pope excommunicated him for smashing the statues in the churches and tearing down wayside crosses. So Gowther took to the forest and became a brigand. He became master of all the savage wastes. However, mixing with the she-bears and the wolves, he committed so many crimes in the woods and on the clifftops that his father had to call him back home to keep a watch on his misdeeds. With the aim of keeping an eye on his son, he offered him a château above Rouen. He dubbed him knight. Yet nothing managed to restrain the violence within Gowther. In tournaments, as soon as he had knocked them to the ground with his lance, he beheaded all the nobles.

It came to the point where none of them would fight him, sure as they were of losing their faces.

From the outer fringes of Brittany to the plains of the Ile-de-France, this meant an end to the tournaments that had been the life of the old world.

°The last tournament to take place in Normandy was held at Arques.

A particularly large crowd assembled in the bushes, with the children along the edge of the meadow and the women sheltering beneath the shade of the trees in the wooded groves. Yet only one horse was seen on the heath. Only Sir Gowther rode out to do battle. The air was blank and empty. None of the Norman nobility came forward to fight him. The crowd, weary of waiting, scattered on to the paths and into the hawthorn bushes. At the end of the day Sir Gowther and his valets, drunk with wine and fired with rage purely from being deprived of an outlet for their violence, turned on the abbey that lay beside the field of Arques where the tourney should have taken place. They persecuted the abbott, abbess, gardeners and nuns, and for six days had their way with them all—even devouring some of them.

Gowther burnt down the abbey of Arques.

Sir Gowther made no attempt to excuse his actions. He said an inner demon, speaking very loudly inside him, had told him: 'No to Good. No to sleep. No to music. No to images. No to books. No to chess-boards.'

On his return from Arques, he felt desire for his mother.

His terrified mother, her shift torn and soiled, stretched out before him on the floor, her face pressed to the ground and her hands clasped together, told him in hushed tones of the secret of his conception. He heard her and was still. He drew out his sword in the darkness and with it cut off his own hair. He went over to the arrow slit in the castle wall and threw his sword into the moat. He left the castle wearing only his shirt, fell to his knees, crossed Gaul on his knees, went to Marabode, saw the pope.

'I am the son of the Duke of the Normans,' he announced to him. 'My mother, weary of praying to

God, once offered her womb to a demon from the other world, and I emerged from it in conditions I shall now relate to you.'

'Do not! Never open your mouth again, my son! That is an order. What a bane your arrival on earth has been! What a greater bane your coming to the Eternal City, where God has demanded of me that I rule the surface of this world! Never more open your mouth, my son! It is your Holy Father who commands it!'

From that day onward, in obedience to the pope, Gowther did not speak again.

The pope entrusted the now wholly mute Gowther, knees bloodied and head shaven, to a hermit whom he venerated. The anchorite, who was very old, lived towards the top of a steep hill in the Roman countryside above Orte. The hermit provided him with a little bread each day to keep his stomach working. That was all. Then he went back to his rocks. Gowther rose at prime but left his bread to the dogs, whose ordure he ate even before it had entirely left their anuses, so pious had he become. One day the anchorite told his disciple:

'I am grown very old. Go back to the city of Rome. I must give you your penance before my soul is spirited away into the other world. At Rome do not seek out the pope. Go on behaving in a manner that causes all who meet you to hate you, beat you, defile you, curse you. Remain dumb. Go on living on all fours. Go on abstaining from all food and drink, except that of dogs or chickens.'

At Rome he dined on the filth of animals, the mud of paths and riverbanks, the monthly excrements of women, the linen of nurslings, vegetable waste, cast-off shoes, cow's lungs, old matting. When the Saracens, aided by Turkish nobles, attacked Rome, an angel approached the kennel where Robert (this is the Latin form of Gowther) lay resting against the side of a bitch. The angel was very small. He was barely one-foot tall. The angel offered Gowther a white horse measuring twenty hands, a white lance over twelve-feet long, a truly tiny white shield (an inch by an inch-and-a-half) and a silver sword. Thus equipped, Sir Gowther smashed the Muslim armies. Three times he fought them. Each battle left not a man standing nor a horse alive. At the end of these battles, after each victory, the hero who had accomplished these feats was never found. Within Rome's ramparts he passed unnoticed, as he fought on all fours in the alleyways with dogs over bones, or was serviced by them, had taunts heaped upon him, was covered in vomit or beaten, still in the same posture.

It so happened that the daughter of the Roman king had overheard his dealings with the little angel but, unfortunately for her, the princess was dumb from birth. She could not, therefore, tell anyone of the mysterious conversations to which she had been privy from the top of her tower. On the last day, after the final victory, she came down from the tower. She walked out on to the ramparts. Holding up her skirts and princess' robes, she went down among the dogs. She offered herself to Gowther in the ditch, indicating to him by signs that she knew who had performed the heroic exploits that had occurred in the battle. He refused her offer. With no regard for her own shame and desirous of a child by him, the princess undressed completely. He averted his eyes. Then, with her fingers, the Roman princess parted the lips of her vulva, so that the conqueror of the Turks might enter and make her pregnant with a little angel. Gowther, still without saying a word, turned his back on her and immediately left the Eternal City. He died deep in the woods, having returned to his master's hermitage, gnawing on the bones of his master who had died in the meantime. With his teeth, he cracked open the bones, sucked out the marrow and buried it in his soul.

CHAPTER 15

La Valliote was the baroque world's most beautiful woman. She was also Paris' greatest tragedian. Her real name was Élisabeth Dispanet. Her beauty alone would have been enough to fill the theatres. She acted in the Prince of Orange's company for seven years, then in 1626 joined the French King's Players. She gave herself to all the nobles. Her career ended when the abbot of Armentières married her and took her out of the theatre. Though she was not exactly sixteen any longer, he forced her to sleep by his side without a nightgown. When she died, he was so mad about his wife's body that he kept her skull. He had the flesh removed and the skull painted black. He placed it in his bedchamber on a writing desk with colonnette legs, so that he could go on sleeping by its side. He said that, when sleep would not come, he could still murmur to her in the night, evoke memories and speak of happy times.

CHAPTER 16

Anne de Lenclos was twenty years old in 1640. A virtuoso on the lute and theorbo, she was honest and prodigiously pale of complexion. She had a fine voice, a narrow-waisted body in the Japanese style and big black eyes. She was a fine dancer and spoke and read the Italian and Spanish languages. Anne de Lenclos preferred to be called Ninon. She said, 'Love is a sentiment that implies no merit in the person who arouses it. It requires no gratitude or grateful acknowledgement from us, since what is in play is a will that is not our own. That is what love is—unexpected longing, worthy of distaste and a prisoner to time.'

*

When on the brink of death, Henri de Lenclos had his daughter come to him:

'Daughter, I think you should take heed only of time. Never have any qualms about number, age, rank, cost, aspect or circumstance—only about the choice of object at the time you will enjoy it.'

'Forgive me for seizing the opportunity here, Father. Do you really believe that these two French words have a meaning when they are pronounced next to each other: *je jouis*—I climax?'

'I think we must do as the clouds do. We must pretend to say: I rain.'

'But you, Father, you who were so good as to "rain" me once upon a time, do you really believe this?'

No answer.

Dying at more than eighty years of age, Ninon de Lenclos said: 'If anyone had offered me such a life, however they might have done so, I would have hanged myself.'

She said 'hanged'. She did not say 'decapitated'.

*

Fifty years after her death, it was the fashion at the French court to keep a skull about you. When your inner sense of lamentation dried up or the pangs of remorse faltered, you contemplated it. The Jesuit fathers asserted that such contemplation could suffice for prayer. To stroke a skull was worth a prayer in the eyes of God. These lifeless craniums were adorned with coifs or with little lights to make them more attractive. °Queen Marie Leszczyńska had asked for the skull of Ninon de Lenclos to be placed on her writing desk. The Marquis d'Argenson, the commissary for war, reports that she thrummed on it from time to time, saying, 'Now, my pretty!'

*

It is either the case that—after her death and before her burial—Ninon was beheaded or that her tomb was desecrated, her body exhumed, what remained of her bones broken apart and her skull removed, cleaned, whitened and handed over to the queen of France.

Those who have not lived in the eighteenth century know nothing of the sweetness of life.

CHAPTER 17

Eternal Damnation

ºMaubert is a contraction of Maître Albert (Master Albert), which in turn refers to Albertus Magnus. Albertus Magnus said that damnation was the worst aspect of hell. There are three infernal punishments: the punishment of the Senses, of Eternity and of Damnation. The punishment of the Senses consists in the intensity of suffering experienced by the five senses. The punishment of Eternity consists in the infinity of suffering, once it becomes limitless and irremediable. The punishment of Damnation is the soul's loss of God—the loss of Paradise, of the maternal, of inherence, of consolation, of rest and return.

The damnation of all human beings is this loss. 'I am lost'—these are the words of the damned man.

In Persian, damnation is *duzokh*, which means 'time stops passing'. For the damned, the Eternal has said: 'Three days last a thousand years.' This is damnation—arrested time.

There are illnesses in which time no longer exists. An old woman sits on the edge of her bed. Her legs dangle. With her nightdress crumpled up round her waist you can see the little white hairs around her sex. She has tears in her eyes. Her white chignon is undone. Her back sobs noiselessly.

You had to approach her gently. You had to touch her hands first, to reassure her by stroking her hands. Then you could dress her again.

CHAPTER 18

Bellerophon was the first melancholy hero of the ancient Greek world.

°Homer says of him in the Iliad: 'But when Bellerophon, at last, himself / Had anger'd all the Gods, feeding on grief / He roam'd alone the Aleian field, exiled, / By choice, from every cheerful haunt of man.' The whole of melancholy is contained in these lines written or dictated by Homer. Persecution, isolation, asymbolia, misanthropy. And, above all, that heart which sadness devours like a wild beast hounding its prey. The autophagia of unhappiness. I am a man of the Old Country. I have never been able to prevent myself from replying 'present' when the sudden call of solitude and silence has come—that call which is always raised for me by the presence of shouting, screaming, jabbering, angrily stamping humanity, as it advances in nations to kill, or gathers in disorganized crowds to see killing done. Rare are the times when I haven't rashly hastened my departure. Those who see me slipping away in a trice wrongly suppose that this sudden flight is the product of anxiety. It is worse than anxiety: it is the sense of humanity.

Solitudo is an old Latin word that meant wilderness.

The call of solitude is one of the most irresistible voices that societies addressed to men from the earliest times.

Solitude is a universal experience. That experience is older than social life, for the whole of the first part of life, in the first kingdom, was a solitary life.

Saint Augustine wrote: 'Life before birth was an experience.'

In Chinese, the words 'reading' and 'alone' are homophones.

Alone with Alone.

Opening a book, he opened his door to the dead and welcomed them in. He no longer knew whether he was on earth or not.

CHAPTER 19

The Last Abbot

In 840 CE, the district governor came to inspect the monasteries of the province of the North. Abbot Obaku hid nothing from the governor. He gave him all his administrative files and accounts, not holding back a single item. He answered all the questions the governor put to him. He had him shown round all the rooms. He opened all the storerooms to him. When they reached the Great Hall of the monastery, in which were displayed the portraits of the various abbots who had succeeded one another since the monastery's foundation, at last they all sat down, forming a semicircle, contemplating the wall. They were silent at first. Then the district governor pointed to the portrait of the last abbot that was hanging on the wall. He asked the abbot softly: 'Where is that man?'

'That is our late abbot,' replied Obaku.

But the governor pressed the point, raising his voice:

'I can see his portrait. I knew him when he was alive. I know that he is dead. The portrait is a lifelike one. But where is he?'

The abbot did not know how to reply.

The district governor now began to shout, asking his question a second time:

'Where is he?'

In his embarrassment, Abbot Obaku turned to the monks around him, so that they might come to his aid.

Each of them lowered his eyes, not knowing what to say.

The district governor now screamed out his question, asking it a third time.

The monks all kept their heads bowed between their knees.

Silence fell in the Hall of Portraits. It became painful.

The governor, stubborn and inscrutable, did not attempt to break the silence. The father abbot suddenly remembered a strange monk who had recently arrived at the monastery and spent his time sweeping the courtyard. He was presented to the district governor. The governor greeted him and said:

'Venerable one, these gentlemen present do not deign to reply to a question I am asking myself. Will you be so good as to do so in their stead?'

'What is your question?'

'I see this man in front of you. I see who he is. This is the portrait of the late abbot, who preceded Mr Obaku in his functions and whom I loved. But where is he?'

The monk mumbled: 'Oh, Governor!'

The governor replied: 'Yes, Venerable one.'

The monk looked at him and, in hushed tones, asked: 'Where are you, Governor?'

Having uttered these words, the monk began gently sweeping the tiled floor in front of him.

Then the district governor blushed.

He got up. He bowed low before the venerable monk. He thanked him. He begged him to make him a present of the broom he was holding in his hands. The venerable monk refused to hand over his broom. The district governor commanded that a celebratory service be held in honour of the monk with the broom. The following night, Abbot Obaku went into the forest and hanged himself from an acacia tree. In the morning, before the sun was up, the rooks had already eaten his ears.

CHAPTER 20

In the magnificent chateau they had had built near the former capital of the kingdom of the Franks, the device of the Clermont family was carved over each window and on the pediment of each door: *Si omnes ego non.* If all, not I. If everyone is there without exception, then I at least will be an exception. Family affiliates faces. Society subjects subjects. The volume of the 'public thing' (*res publica*) has increased with the making-public and normalizing of all 'private' things (*res privata*): upbringing, conscience, knowledge, sickness, married life, old age and death. Even the foetus is photographed *in utero*. This is the surveillance of all within each. *Omnis* dominates *Ego*.

*

Pindar wrote in his second Pythian ode: *Genoi autos essi mathon*. Become what you are. No, do not become what you are. What individualizes is the proper name or, in other words, the language in which it has its place—that is to say, social control through the internalized voice or, in other words, endless servitude. Do not become the slave of your people in the patronym they gave you within the collective language they taught you. Otherwise, the name they gave you will take the place of your flesh.

Do not become *autos*. Do not become the same as you. Do not become an *idem*. For *idem* is not *ipse*. Do not become *your*self but become *the* self, the *sich*, the *sui*, the sacred intimate object, the incommunicable portion, the Erstwhile.

Egoism is, perhaps, an unrealizable project for humans who speak. In the decisions we take, we harm ourselves like those birds of prey that smash the eggs of their own broods. What is the 'every man for himself' formula worth, if everyone hates himself? Inwardness was invented by the voice of the mother before coming to be inhabited, much later, by everyone's voices. But the voice that could be said to be 'personal' is one no one hears. In truth, the depth of the body does not know inwardness.

Do not become what you are. Do not become *autos*. Do not become *idem*. Do not try to be different from the others, because the desire to be different from the others is what the world dictates. To be so is to adapt yourself to the ways of the majority and of one's rivals. To try to be interesting is to want to be identified. Do not try to be interesting. Do not identify yourself with anything. Do not become identical with yourself. Do not go towards yourself. For no one has genuinely reached the most impulsive element of the inner rhythm that governs him, the most autonomous aspect of what is alive in his life, because we are all children. We are all, men or women, off-shoots of women. We were housed in them. We are all fascinated creatures, imitators, taught beings, thieves. The whole of the language in us, being something stolen rather than originally present, is the language of a liar. We have no core. This is what neoteny means: we are animals without instinct. That the national language is acquired means that everything which enables us to differentiate ourselves is acquired.

Far upstream from the two kingdoms, our 'substance' cannot be very different from erogenous openings and temporal incompletions. Mouth, eyes, anus, ears, nostrils—every human being is holed with that animality which he would like to slough off. Chuang-Tzu says that all openings are points of incompletion. Chuang-Tzu wrote: 'Men project their nine orifices on to the earth and into the heavens.'

CHAPTER 21

Ipsimus

In ancient Rome the master was called *Ipsimus* by the slaves. If *ipse* means himself, the superlative of *ipse* refers to a 'more himself than all himselves'. In this way, the superlative of domination defines within its name the servility over which it gains ascendancy. In social life, extreme dependency on the extreme identity of the master is granted, on a continuous basis, by the 'subjects', who have renounced all personal life. Every little human is a subject (*ego*), as soon as he subjects himself, of his own accord, by acquiring the language of the community.

This is the soul as obedience and as faith.

Why is rebellion always both so incredibly easy and so incredibly rare?

The Romans' *ipsimus* is the foundation for the persecuting 'He'. The 'He' in which the paranoid believe, as they believe in their fathers. This wild *ipsimus* becomes the tyrant of autocratic societies. This divine *ipsimus* becomes the majority in democratic societies. 'They say that I . . .', 'They want me to . . .', 'They think that I . . .'. This is no longer even an admitted *egophoria*, dispensing language into the heart of the one using it, but *doxa* become *ipsima*. It is the opinion of all become the rule. It is the 'law of the market' become desire. It is the endless opinion poll. It is the voting forecasts that precede the elections and bring about an even bloodier 'massacre'. Men, surely you are not going to deprive yourselves endlessly of everything in order to feed the Inca, Pharaoh, God or the emperor Napoleon. But human societies have no wish to leave behind the religion that intoxicates them, that sets them against one another, that lends its magic to the wars which, in turn, endlessly fuel their excitement and amplify their faith.

To turn one's back on society, to break off from believing, to turn away from anything to do with looking and to prefer reading to surveillance, to protect those who have passed on from the survivors who denigrate them, to give succour to what is not visible—these are the virtues. The rare ones who have the matchless courage to escape spring up out in the wilds.

CHAPTER 22

Separate, Sacred Communication

When we cry out for the first time in the light of the day, we carry with us the loss of a dark, voiceless, solitary, liquid world. That place and that silence will never be ours again. A dark cave, underground chambers, shadows from before ourselves, dark banks and a sodden shore haunt men's souls always and everywhere. All viviparous animals have their lair. It is the idea of a place that could be said to be not just mine but myself in person.

We are talking of a place before a body.

The intimacy that has the oldest of our worlds lying inside ourselves is the rarest treasure.

Always a little personal confidence that we shall divulge to no one, that we shall not even necessarily admit to ourselves, saves us.

Whoever has a secret has a soul.

*

A scene of nudity, more or less embarrassing and mysteriously nocturnal, surrounded by lamp brackets, surrounded by candles, surrounded by torch holders, is to be found long before the bodies it produces. A non-communication from far before communication must be preserved in the atmospheric world. It is a reserve of wild animality that must never subject itself to language, nor to the arts, nor to the community, nor to the family, nor become part of lovers' secrets.

A clinical recess, as it were, of the individual soul.

The heart of every woman and man must be regarded as unexploitable.

It must on no account be discovered by the others, nor arouse their desire, nor be glimpsed by the other wild beasts or the birds, nor be stolen or devoured.

*

Kryptadia—this was the name scholars gave in the past to anthologies of sexual folklore. They went down into the cellars of the main body of the palace; they hid the apotropaic images their forefathers had fashioned in a 'secret museum'. That was what happened at Naples. Or they went up into the attic of the Palais Mazarin; they closed the door of a Labrouste iron cupboard behind them, pretending it was the subterranean world of the shades, hiding their scandalous origins. This was what happened at Paris.

This iron cupboard, which they called *Enfer* or Hell, was like a safe situated amid the beauty of the old books, in which they hid their shame.

Books open up the imaginary space, a space that is itself primal, where each singular being is brought back up against the contingency of his animal source and the untameable instinct that causes living creatures to reproduce.

Books may be dangerous but it is reading above all, in and of itself, that spells danger.

Reading is an experience that entirely transforms those who devote their souls to it. You have to keep real books tightly in a corner, for real books always stand out against collective mores. He who reads lives alone in his 'other world', in his little 'nook', his corner of the wall. In this way, the reader is the only being in society who physically, solitarily confronts, in the book, the abyss of the prior solitude in which he lived. Simply, by merely turning the pages of his book, he endlessly brings back before himself the (sexual, familial and social) rift from which he issues.

°Every reader is like Saint Alexis beneath his father's stairs. He has become as silent as the bowl that is brought to him.

Only the letter placed in front of his lips can attest that he breathes no more.

In written expression by means of letters, without there being any need to articulate them, something manages to make itself understood.

He who reads the letter has lost self, name, filiation and earthly life.

In literature something reverberates from the other world.

Something of the secret is handed on.

*

We began as a secret for no one—dumb, embryonic, in the dark. Where is the crowd in our mothers' wombs? There are seven solitudes. The first solitude is foetal solitude. We do not start out in a world lit like an airport departure lounge. In the course of our first life we know nothing, not only of torches but of the stars. Even the sun is unknown to us in our first experience of life. Later, remembering this first sojourn, we dream alone, deliberately re-immersing our bodies each night in a darkness we create artificially, by pulling curtains or closing shutters. This is nocturnal solitude. Every ninety minutes, three or four times a night, a rhythm as regular as a rising tide sends images to us that we do not understand. Slow sleep defines the time of cellular re-synchronization. 'Paradoxical' sleep is the name for the realm of descent into neuronal anarchy, mental anachrony, genital erection. Anachrony is to time what anchoretism is to the group. Only the synchronization of time and effort is addressed to the day, to the family, to society, to language, to the nation, to one's mother's applause, to the master's joy, to acclamation from the majority, to the greater glory of God. Wishes are not. Hunger is not. Desire is not. Vows are not. Fantasies are not. At night, the solitary dream raises or dilates the sex organ, which is what solitarizes the body of the—male or female—sleeper. The vital secret—such is sexual solitude. What the hand spontaneously hides in fear is this 'alone', this strange monotheism placed in the centre of the body. The pleasure termed 'solitary' passes from oneiric erection to childhood masturbation. Then comes the passionate, assiduous, faithful *manustupratio*, parallel with heterosexual curiosity and specific to the genital phase. Solitude then forever arrays a world in which to shelter and renounce obedience. This is solitude as radical prayer. It is solitude in the sense of the worship of the loss of sociality, the disinhibiting of *doxa*, collective unfettering. What the monks of the Palestinian desert called prayer is perhaps closer to what we moderns call thought. In prayer, breath becomes solitude. In prayer, language becomes foreign. This is what I call reading and all reading is social solitude. Benedikt Spinoza: 'Man is happy only in solitude, where he obeys only himself.' Marx: 'We have nothing to lose but our chains.' The sixth solitude is the solitude of death throes. Cats that are dying, humans who are dying, dogs that are dying, spontaneously set themselves apart. And, moreover, those who remain among the humans take their distance from the dying man before death occurs; they leave him alone in his extreme solitude; terror in the face of the corpse opens up a space of solitude; this is in itself an imaginary hole opening up in space; an absence adding itself to what has already withdrawn; a place at which to dig, at which to bury. The solitude of silence is the solitude of the abandonment of language within language. Not to speak to oneself when alone (*soliloquium*) but to feel oneself alone on the basis of the most complete silence. Wilfred Bion: 'The capacity to be alone is the aim of life. It is the basis of creativity.' °Melanie Klein: 'To feel alone is the programme.'

*

Because solitude precedes birth, we should not defend society as a value:

Non-society is the aim.

Thought is constantly running up against the limits to which its source constrains it and its pain subjects it.

The word infancy is extraordinary. It comes from the Latin *in-fantia* and means inability to speak. It refers to an initial, non-social state that constitutes a source in each of us, in which we have not yet acquired our language. We are non-speaking substance which must learn language from the lips of those close to us. Thus, whatever we learn by living, growing old and working, we are always flesh in which language falters. We are always former in-fants, former non-speakers, viviparous animals, two-world beings in whom language is neither natural nor sure. There is a solitude anterior to narcissism; a terrible infant ecstasy; a forsakenness; a desolation that marks our earliest days; it is almost an internal ecstasy from before ecstasy, from before contemplation, from before reading. This abyssal ecstasy deep inside us can be radicalized to the point of autism. A catastrophic melancholy precedes consciousness, folding the soul back on to it in a closed circuit. I am speaking of the inner world before it is affected by meaningful, acquired, significant, national language. In temporal terms, this melancholic state precedes the formation of consciousness. It precedes identity. If consciousness defines language looping back on itself, then the body must have had the time to consent to the maternal sound world, then acquire it, for there to be retroaction, then reflection, then self-apprehension. One must have lived at least two years. This closed circuit before consciousness is the space of a secret. A rebirth and a recognition of this internal ecstasy—this is what reading is. The reader may adore this *vertige*— or the person who refuses to read may detest it—for this *vertige* was at their source.

The specific characteristic of orgasm is temporal—it is the loss of the consciousness of time as duration.

This characteristic is also that of reading.

I am here evoking bodies totally 'in the grip' of the other world. It is the impossible homecoming to the inner world I am speaking of. The impossible restoration of consonance with the container. The madness of the 'loop'. It is also the madness of love: to believe it is *possible* to re-find the instantaneous communication of one being with another.

In the last interview he gave before his death, before being knocked down by a van as he was crossing the road, Roland Barthes stated that independent

life was going to become a real challenge in democratic societies. He added that the person who sought
to live out his indivisibility radically would be
embarking on a very difficult life. °He would be setting out on an adventure as engimatic as that faced
by most of the knights in the old Breton tales as they
ventured into the dangerous forest. It is true that this
attitude is in conflict nowadays not only with the
mode of life of the youngest groups but with the general operation of surveillance, with moral solidarity,
with collective health, with science and its networks
of authorization and validation. Roland Barthes said
expressly: 'The one thing a power never tolerates is
contestation through withdrawal. That can only be
done by clandestine behaviour. By cheating. You can
confront a power by attacking it. A society finds withdrawal much less easy to assimilate.'

Love defines this 'that': separate, sacred communication, the secret life, intense life apart from society,
the family and common language. In the finest novel
of love written in France, *La Châtelaine de Vergy*, love
is described as the relationship that excludes any inter-
vention from a third party; that excludes any divulging

of confidences; that imposes the secrecy of the lair. It is the same in the finest novel of love written in Great Britain, *Wuthering Heights*. In the Breton legends, secrets cannot be told. Lovers' secrets cannot be divulged, even to the air, without bringing down disasters. They must be revealed only in writing, must never reach anyone's ear, must be concealed from nature and from all classes of society.

*

0'*S'il vous plaît nous laissez écrire*
Ce que de bouche n'osons dire.'

CHAPTER 23

The Countess of Hornoc had black eyes. Her hair was black. She was thin and hirsute. She had long, black body hair that had never been cut or shaved. She was rich. In the month of December 1615, the winter solstice banquet was given at Antwerp in honour of the New Year. Her mother being no longer of this world, it fell to the Countess of Hornoc to preside over it, alongside her grandmother. She wanted to be the most beautiful person there. She was a violent woman. She ordered a dress of purple velvet, a large gold necklace and a gold ring with a figure of a horse on it.

She said: 'It is the winter sun.'

Everything was done as she wished. The goldsmith alone was found wanting, receiving a blow on the back of his hand with his stamp because he had forgotten a leg in the figure of the tiny jumping horse.

The day of the solstice celebration arrived. At dawn the countess had a starcher sent to her. She chose to have the neck folded down in two tiny pleats, but she was not happy with the girl's work. When she tried to show her that the two folds were not exactly parallel, the girl, herself very quick-tempered, answered back. They fought. The countess bit the starcher on the back of the neck, tearing away a lump of flesh. Blood spurted from the wound. She had to be restrained. Her family impressed upon her that she should not behave like this. But the young countess would have nothing of it. They made her drink a herbal tea. They made her lie down. They cared for the starcher as best they could, since strange visions had begun to torment her, and they took her home.

An older dressmaker was called. She was, actually, the one who had made the purple dress. She was an old woman, slow and phlegmatic, who had caused no problems when the dress had been made. The young countess, now pressed for time, decided on an almond-shaped gore with a single pleat, fringed with pearls. But when the old woman sewed it round her neck, the countess did not like it. They had words. Just how it came about that she beat the woman to death is not known. Or, rather, the old woman fell after receiving a first few slaps. Thereafter, the Countess of Hornoc trampled what remained of her body underfoot. They brought the grandmother down, carrying her in their arms. She looked at the body of the old dressmaker on the floor, her limbs all awry and assumed that her granddaughter had gone mad.

The old countess immediately ordered a doctor to be sent for. Within moments, a man presented himself at the drawing-room door. A white-haired gentleman. They asked if he was a doctor. He answered, yes. What was his name? Monsieur de Hel. He wore a golden doublet, a golden baldric and yellow hose. The curious thing was that there was a great deal of mud on his golden boots. He lifted up the trampled dressmaker, who suddenly began to moan in his arms. He laid her out gently on the window bench. Sunlight fell on the old woman's face. 'You are the sun,' she said and began to breathe again. He sat her up gently on the window bench. The Hornocs' steward approached the stranger and said to him: 'Monsieur de Hel, I doubt you are a doctor. You are a creature from the Other world.'

'I am neither,' he replied to the steward. 'I am a tailor.'

'Your clothes are so magnificent.'

'I hope so. If I wear magnificent clothing, it is to advertise what I can produce with my needle.'

The young Countess of Hornoc said at once:

'We have need of a tailor. This woman, who five minutes ago was dead, was a dressmaker.'

'You are wearing a ring that gives you pain.'

'What do you know of my ring? For my part, I can see that you are a nobleman.'

'What makes you say that?'

'I know you are noble because you are wearing a baldric.'

'It is true I have a horse, and yet I am a tailor.'

'Are you from the north of Flanders?'

But he took the hand of the young Countess of Hornoc, who was surprised by the action, and spent some time examining her ring, which bore the figure of a horse, on its hind legs, in the act of jumping.

The young countess began to tremble.

Then he let go of her hand and, lifting his handsome blue eyes, said:

'I'm hungry.'

The tailor then pointed at the floor to the pleated collars that had been trampled.

The young countess suddenly grew calm.

She looked at him in astonishment.

He announced: 'I'm going to make the ruff you wanted from your dressmaker before you wounded her, while attempting to send her to her death.'

This he did. The young Countess of Hornoc watched him without saying another word. The ruff, with a golden thread running through it, was of a beauty almost beyond description. He sowed it on to the young woman's neck himself. Seeing the countess, one would have thought her a queen or a saint. In five minutes it was done.

'It isn't a ring,' he added. 'It's a collar.'

But the young countess seemed dumbstruck. She gazed at him in silence.

He looked her in the eyes and said: 'I repeat that I am hungry.'

She led him in person to the kitchens.

*

It fell to the Countess of Hornoc to dance the opening dance with the alderman. As she danced, she gradually came to feel the ruff strangling her. But little by little, something happened that made her blush. As her collar tightened, she felt the lips of her sex distend with each new dance step she must take. She had to dance with the leading councillors of the city of Antwerp, each in their turn.

Her juices began gradually to flow. She could see this by the marks she left on the floor as she danced and was embarrassed by it. She scanned the room, eventually meeting the eyes of Seigneur de Hel, who was standing in the doorway. He was magnificent. He was wearing a golden doublet. He had a golden baldric around his waist, which fell over his yellow hose. However, his boots were rather dirty, as though he had been walking in the country or along the banks of a pond. Behind him, through the windows that lay open on to the river Scheldt, one could see the night and the masts of the ships. The moon shone on the port. The moonlight glistened on all the little waves that crashed against the flanks of the vessels. The moonlight gleamed on the great waves rising round their hulls.

He doffed his hat.

His white locks appeared, haloed in mist.

The young countess abandoned her dancing partner.

She went leszczyńska him.

He did not move towards her but simply reached out his hands.

She placed her two hands in his.

He mumbled: 'Your cheeks are red.'

The young woman's two hands were burning.

'It so happens that your ruff is squeezing my neck and my juices are flowing.'

'I'll let it out . . .'

'No, leave it please. I want you.'

Her desire was stronger. She had taken his hand. She could feel her vulva palpitating between her legs.

'Come, come,' she said.

They went out onto the terrace. She took him behind the northern sentry post. She rummaged in his hose.

She bared a long, yellow, smooth, stiff sex.

Moisten as the countess' sex might, it was extraordinarily narrow. Only after several attempts did Seigneur de Hel succeed in penetrating her. When she began to climax, she thrust her red tongue between his lips but the nobleman wouldn't open his mouth and the countess couldn't get her tongue into it.

She did not even manage to cry out.

She did not even manage to get her breath back.

She suddenly fell over in the dark night.

*

In the morning when they went to look for the young Countess of Hornoc in the grounds, they found her stretched out on the terrace behind the door of the sentry post. Her fulsome dress was pulled up over her skinny legs. They went up to her. They cried out. They removed the ruff. They undid her dress. They tried to apply pressure to her stomach and ribs to make her breathe but they were unable to revive her. They looked for the tailor. They found neither man nor horse. Everyone was happy that the young countess had perished. They made a banquet of the previous day's leftovers.

CHAPTER 24

Whitcomb Judson

A New Englander invented an extraordinary two-part clothing fastener of gilded metal. In naming it, he used a comparison borrowed from lightning as it fell from the sky. He said: 'I shall call you "lightning fastener".'

His name was Whitcomb Judson. He put it on sale in the early months of 1891.

Homer and Pindar termed the fragments of the token that were broken when heroes parted *'symbola'*. On their return, after years had passed, the heroes fitted the two edges together. At the point where their piece of the puzzle fitted exactly into the other, eyes recognized faces.

In just the same way, the rat stands stock-still, recognizing the dentition of the snake that frighteningly haunted his dreams, even before he had perceived it in reality.

He seems enraptured.

At that point, beneath the snake's tooth, the rat becomes the larger form of the Erstwhile which awaited him in space and which he had seen in the night.

By the end of 1891, Mr Judson's hook-and-eye fastener had found eleven buyers.

In 1892, there were twenty-two.

In 1893, thirty-three.

In 1894, forty-four.

In 1900, a hundred.

In 1901, Whitcomb Judson put the Universal Fastener Company into voluntary liquidation.

In 1909, as Whitcomb Judson lay dying, his wife came into his bedroom and he took her hand in his. He squeezed it very tightly. He asked if she remembered that he had once had the idea, almost twenty years ago, that if he put two gold, toothed racks together, the one running counter to the other, the teeth would stay locked together. His invention was now nothing but a stupid name, redolent of storms.

CHAPTER 25

Ecstasy and Enstasy

In calling solitude a 'prayer' and that prayer a 'reading', I am evoking an extreme form of polarization.

This is what the Greek mystics called an ecstasy.

In Greek 'mystic' simply means silent.

In Greek 'ecstasy' simply means displacement.

Initially, the trance rises up, dances, spins.

Two fragments of time are suddenly polarized but *ecstasy never sees its own collapse.* It is the same as with desire, which does not see itself climax, because sensual pleasure annihilates it and leaves you without a memory of the preceding state of lack. This is like the dreamer who doesn't see himself dream. Like the mind of the reader, which doesn't see his body reading but has already left to sojourn in the world the plot tells of, to ride or sail around that world. An ecstasy in which polarity is reinforced to the point where it forms an axis (orienting time vertically), setting *up* time (the two positions of the male sex organ ground the bipedal version of time). Ecstasy then . finds itself on the verge of enstasy; time being irreversibility, reversal is lethal to it; Orpheus cannot turn round without, by that mere retroversion, inventing death; time cannot retrace its footsteps; the diver cannot leap back to the top of the cliff. In sudden reversibility, time would be broken. This is why bereavement disorients the survivor so violently. Mad desire is, strictly speaking, *caught in a dizzying whirl*, each of the poles fusing in the impossible, insane to-ing and fro-ing between two souls with distinct sexes—in both directions, in all directions. This to-and-fro arrow is the invention of the boomerang. In the Japanese version, the present grows and grows by a ceaseless inflow from the past. Since the origins, the waves of time have become more and more voluminous, whiter and whiter, taller and taller, more and more violent. Physicists say of black holes that, as a result of concentrating in the night sky, they roll up space into their dark substance and pour it out into time. Without realizing it, what physicists are describing here is the rotation that occurs in nervous breakdowns, which is simply the impossible regression of children from the woman they face, as they speak, to the mother who carried them when it was not possible for them to speak.

CHAPTER 26

Impetuous Death

The magnificent, liquid word 'suicide' emerged in the heart of the baroque world. Up to that point, French legal scholars and priests with their Latin employed circumlocution. They spoke of 'self-inflicted' or 'impetuous' death. Religion and superstition no doubt didn't wish this decisive act to become a common noun. By denying it a place in the dictionary, they hoped, perhaps, to drive the sin out of reality. But what was Lancelot doing when, believing Guinevere to be dead, he tied a rope to the pommel of his saddle? What was Roland doing in his rocky recess at Roncevaux, renouncing flight and refusing surrender? In order to designate 'the homicide of someone who is not a third party', the theologians of the Church of Rome formed a Latin word by adding *sui* and *caedes* together. Literally: of oneself the murder. In 1652 Caramuel entitled a chapter of his *Theologia moralis fundamentalis* 'De suicidio'—on suicide. The word was employed first in England, then in France and Italy, before reaching Spain.

CHAPTER 27

De Suicidio

Martin Heidegger wrote, as readily as Phocion before him, that no one can take another's dying from him. You can take a man's life but, in the death of the man being killed, you cannot take his dying from him. Heidegger's phrase combines death as possibility and death as abduction. It is understandable only if man is first conceived as hostage to the strange abduction of death.

Scholium I. This abduction into 'imprehensible dying' is time. Paradoxically, what humans call death is a second, imitated predation, which remembers the murder of prey.

Scholium II. This *raptus* that is *possibilitas* provides the ground for suicide in man. Suicide refers to murder done on oneself. What does it mean to speak of murder concerning the self? *Sui-caedes*? Murderer of self? This means no one can steal the 'possibility' of his suicide from another.

Corollary. Any human being who dares comment on the death another human being has just dealt himself is a scoundrel.

*

Death is not simply an irreversible feature of birth, since birth does not coincide in humans with life. Death is a primal, inevitable element. No sexed existence can avoid having to think about being conceived; of having lived in a sex organ and having fallen from it in possession of one of the two sexes possible in this world; of having one day to be killed, to die or to kill oneself within that irremediable sex. Death constitutes time neither as a horizon of Being, nor as an origin of Being, nor as the non-being of beings. Death is the time which, inasmuch as 'one day, one will have to die', lies in *jouissance* (the reproduction of new living creatures presupposes the death of the old ones). It is the time that I cannot place in time since it arises in desire. °'But of that day ... knoweth no man'—such is the sensual delight in the end of desire that pours forth in it. On the one side is the 'Once upon a time' of the non-present scene from which the present proceeded, without being and conception being in any way synchronous (presentness derives from birth alone). On the other side of the 'Once upon a time' lies the 'One day, die.' This temporality with two—sexual and mortal—terms to it is absolute. The foetus, the child being born, the autist, the adolescent, the unhappy, the bereaved, the sick, the aged all have the 'One day, die' in them. It is, indeed, that possibility that grants them the line of death as support and non-life as resort.

*

The argument of Epicurus, and subsequently of Lucretius, that death does not exist is a sophism. This argument comes in three forms. When death is there, we are no longer there to meet it. We are never able to face down death as something within us. This argument is wrong because of suicide. Of suicide in general and of the suicide to which Lucretius himself resorted when he could no longer go on. The mortal future is never 'entirely foreign' to us, since death is available to us in an impetuous act. The future is never pure unpredictability since it contains death as possibility. The third and last argument: nothingness is never foreign to man's soul because it precedes our existence. For voluntary death to be chosen, something of the cessation it occasions must, in a sense, be known to those who opt for it. Suicides are, then, dead men who have gone alone to their dying.

*

No one can complain of life: no one is being detained by it. This argument is repeated in the works of the two Senecas, father and son, under Tiberius and Nero. The argument also takes this other form in Rome: the only reason to praise life is that it offers us, alongside itself, the possibility also of extracting ourselves from it. We cannot speak of servitude when emancipation is on offer at the same time. Submission and rebellion are offered together. In hospitals old men hang themselves from their chair arms with the belts of their dressing gowns.

*

To take murder from the wild beasts, to turn it round against oneself, to become one's own wild beast—these are the three phases. Suicide not only breaks the bond of time but breaks the bonds of the human condition.

*

Suicide is 'death lived as dying' when that death proceeds directly from the original distress that lodges in the depths of the body.

The lapsing of human beings from the identical tore the aorist asunder before annihilation.

The apoptosis of the leaves on the trees: they do not so much fall as are carried away by the wind.

Suppression preceded extinction.

CHAPTER 28

There is a strange scene in *The Letters of the Younger Pliny* (Book I, 16), in which a woman 'tests out' death in order to offer it painlessly to her husband. Arria the Elder plunges a dagger beneath her left breast, pulls out the blood-soaked weapon, holds it out to her husband, remains standing and still takes the time to say (though she is dead): '*Non dolet, Paete*' ('It does not hurt, Paetus').

Arria the Elder is not in sync with death.

In the death of Arria the Elder, death does not come.

She is dead and yet, after the spurting of her blood, she once again shows her husband her naked breast, the blade and the possibility of dying.

Arria is the testing out of death.

In the legend of Arria the Elder the only plausible detail is this knife covered with fresh blood which she extracts from her breast and reaches over.

CHAPTER 29

Within 'killing oneself', it is difficult to distinguish between what relates to 'leaving life' and what is about 'leaving the group'.

Political liberty takes four forms. It can be gauged by tyrannicide, violent emancipation, anchoritism and suicide.

To kill oneself is to control annihilation.

What is annihilation? For the content, it is the loss of the container. With viviparous creatures, we are speaking of the loss of the mother. For social beings, it means the loss of society. When Chancellor Hitler began to exercise power, in keeping with the priorities he had outlined in his writings, men committed suicide on the Franco-Spanish border, in a city in Brazil and in a hotel room in New York.

Every man-who-commits-suicide has met his mother-who-is-dying deep within himself.

Since the chain of fascination comes apart and breaks suddenly at adolescence, the desire to die relates particularly to that age.

The infant, having no psychic identity or bodily autonomy, has no possibility of killing himself by his own hand. He either resorts to collapse or calls a truce through anorexia. But if they could, infants wouldn't hesitate to kill themselves. Not possessing the motor capacity, they exploit temporal symmetry (moving in the opposite direction, regressing to the previous stage).

Christian societies forbid suicide as irreligious. Democratic states denounce it as cowardice. Psychiatric societies treat it as an illness. Ancient civilizations praised suicides for their courage. They honoured the act as an act of pride. The ancient Romans said that it was the greatest of the gods, Nature, who, in giving us life, gave us also the possibility of exempting ourselves from the world she engendered. Self-inflicted death is the constant human possibility, always within reach; it is the primary source of aid in suffering; and the split second that is always available for walking out on the group and cutting through time. Horace wrote: *Mors ultima linea rerum.* Death is the ultimate boundary line, from which we can either choose to live or not live in a world. The freedom to kill oneself was lost in Constantine's empire, together with all the individual freedoms. When Christianity took over from imperialism, God became the owner of slavish lives. In reality, in the days of the Republic, all slaves—even soldiers— were already forbidden to commit suicide. In the case of slaves, killing themselves infringed private property rights. For soldiers, doing away with oneself was the equivalent of desertion. In both cases, a breaking of the contract of public service was involved.

It was in 1215 that annual confession was imposed on the faithful to hold despair in check. °Navarrus wrote: 'It is forbidden to kill oneself out of anger, sadness, poverty, sexual shame, physical suffering, any kind of misfortune, excess of pleasure, unwillingness to endure pain or disgust with living. In turning one's hand against oneself, one loses one's place in the cemetery.' Because Christian confession claimed to be able to wrest Satan from the depths of the melancholic body, then dating from its introduction (that is, from the thirteenth century onwards) suicides were interred outside the precincts where the dead were buried.

*

In the world of *ipses* the opposite of the tyrant's *ipsimus* might be said to be the *sui* we find in suicide.

We must leave the bad regions where the gods alone have the right to kill. We must abandon the nations where suicide is forbidden.

Exile and suicide are closely related. Wherever we are, we can desert. We can throw off our exclusive capture by the family and fight against appropriation by society.

Epictetus preferred to say: 'The door is open.'

Epictetus did not say: 'Kill yourself,' but he repeated constantly: 'The door is open.'

One day in Rome, Epictetus, who was the slave of a slave, told this story: 'At the Saturnalia, as a game they draw lots to find a king. The king who has been chosen in this way has command over all those who play along with his pretend kingship. He says, "You, drink. You, mix the wine. You, sing. You, go away. You, come here." They obey in order that the game will not be interrupted. But the door is open. They can leave. Man can leave his life at any moment. He can say, as the king can say in his game, which is his kingdom, "You, go away." '

*

°One day Peter said to Jesus: 'Master, it is good for us to be here.' Now, Jesus replied to Peter: 'No, it is not good for us to be here.'

Light is exile, because we are imprinted with darkness.

Light took nine months to reach beings who knew nothing of it.

Is it possible that the viviparous body, in its dark waters, was awaiting that light?

We have to say no twice here. Language takes twenty-seven months to come. Is it possible that the body, in its crying and its initial dependence, is waiting for it? I pick up the Bible again. The old Latin

Bible I took from my maternal grandmother when she died, alone, on the carpet in the corridor, stretched out in the long, book-lined corridor in the rue Marié-Davy in Paris' fourteenth arrondissement. Deep down, I am still in the rue d'Alésia. I used to go down the rue du Lunain to get to her. I keep turning and turning the pages she endlessly turned in the corner by the window, wetting her finger, her glasses perched on the tip of her nose, a big magnifying glass in her hand. As I do so, I am at her side. I copy and re-copy the mysterious Latin: *Petrus dixit ad Jesum*: *Domine bonum est nos his esse* and suddenly— *repentinum*—I no longer understand what the little word 'here' might mean to a 'viviparous creature'. Aquatic life? Atmospheric life? We are two 'heres' rent apart within ourselves. Two rhythms, cardiac and pulmonary, which are not the same age and are torn in two; rhythms that attempt to harmonize; that do not succeed in harmonizing; that sing. What is the song we are trying to sing? The song is: No, it is not good to be here. We are looking for a here within the here. A woman abandoned us in time. She abandoned us into a separate body. She abandoned us to a sex different from hers. Before this we were in the tepid water of her darkness, to which we shall never return. We opened our eyes with a cry; we stared, wide-eyed; in the light we went astray, etc.

*

Who is the *sui* in sui-cide? I think the English word self in the thought of Donald Winnicott exactly translates the Latin *sui* that figures in the Latin word invented by Caramuel. It is the absence of *ego* that is in *sum*, as it is in *amo*. It is the position before the self-looping circulation of acquired language. That is to say, before the *Ego cogito ergo sum*—in which *sum*, to tell the whole truth, is lost in the *ego* it uncovers.

Ipseity defines the feedback of emotions within the body without the aid of language—that is to say, from far before the ego position.

I suggest that there is already a form of *ipseity* in the life of the foetus.

A withdrawal followed by a reversal. There are already the beginnings of an ecliptic circle in the infant soul. Winnicott thought there was a solitude that preceded narcissism. Melanie Klein thought there was an even older *human desolation*. From our very origins there appears a state verging upon death. We must assume the existence of an ecstasy that might be said to be internal in nature. Lethal ecstasy of the maternal container within the self. This is the instance specific to suicide. The sense of solitude one feels even in friendship, even in sensual delight, comes from the impossible reunion with the *internal* when starting out from the *interior* of the *private* world. It is the impossible restoration of consonance with the container. It is the impossible reinsertion of the content into the container.

*

The madness of the 'loop' is the madness of love: to believe that direct access to the other's *intus* is *possible*. That access took place at conception. There is a communication more rapid than the mediation of the spoken word. It is the madness of reading. Reading is a *possible* reunion with the internal.

*

The old ferryman was quite aged. He was eight thousand years old. He stood up, white-haired, in his bark, leaning on his pole. To all who passed, the boatman said:

'If you see someone in trouble, beware of helping him. He has to come running if you want him to survive.'

*

The impulse towards suicide may be defined as a panic. The panic destruction of the false self to save the true self from annihilation. The suicidal state presupposes the acquisition of language. The false self is the garment patched up with projections and identifications. Superadded are the 'three castrations' that constitute the superego, the *persona* and the false self: the abdication of omnipotence, the sacrifice of bloody violence and the renunciation of individual affirmation. The true self can never obtain a social situation. The place where the true *sui* resides is forever somatic and its communication is silent.

*

Arria the Elder holds out her sword to the man she loves, and speaks after her death.

Cato contemplates his sword.

He used to read in the night.

After reading the *Phaedo* to the very end, he puts the scroll down beside him. He looks for his sword. It is hanging above his bed. He grasps it. He draws the sword from its scabbard. He touches its point. He examines the blade and says: 'Now, I belong to myself.' He picks up Plato's book and begins to read the *Phaedo* again. The birds begin to sing. He suddenly plunges the sword into his belly.

I shall linger a moment over the last word Cato pronounces as he commits suicide. Tradition prefers to highlight the aspects of virility, completeness, belonging: 'Now, I belong to myself.' But what Cato says to himself in Greek—or, rather, the Greek words the Roman hero addresses to his sword before dying—are something much more simple, more archaic, more fundamental: *Nun emos eimi*. 'Now I am mine.' Word for word: Now mine am.

This *emos*, this me that is mine only on the basis of death is the *sui* that is in suicide.

*

Suicide is certainly the ultimate line on which human freedom can be written. It is perhaps its final point. The right to die is not listed among human rights. Just as individualism is not. Just as wild passion is not. As atheism is not. These human possibilities are too extreme. They are too antisocial to be accepted into the code that claims to rule societies. For a man is born a believer the way a rabbit is dazzled by headlights.

If atheism is the outermost point of the individualization of human beings, suicide is the outermost point of human liberty.

*

Brontë, Kleist, Kafka, Proust, Mishima: suicide as work, as fulfilment of the work, as mark of its completion, as full stop.

CHAPTER 30

Jesus the Suicide

Jesus committed suicide. In John 10:18, Jesus says:

'No man taketh [my life] from me (*nemo tollit eam a me vitam*), but I lay it down of myself (*sed ego pono eam a meipso*). I have power to lay it down (*potestatem habeo ponendi eam*).'

In the Greek of John's gospel, Jesus says even more violently:

'No one can wrest my psyche from me. I alone am capable of taking my soul from me.'

CHAPTER 31

Liberty

To the ears of an ancient Greek, the Greek word for liberty (*eleutheria*) meant the possibility of going where one wants (*to elthein opou erâ*). Liberty is what sets the citizen off from the slave, who is cooped up on an agricultural estate, fettered in a manufactory or chained to the oarsmen in a galley.

In the Greek verb *eleusomai* (to go where you want) the wild beasts live again, as opposed to domestic animals, surrounded by fences, walls, barbed wire and boundaries.

In Latin, it is Liber, the god of the vine and eruptive speech, who lies at the bottom of *libertas*. To a Roman, *libertas* means the continuous, progressive, blossoming, luxuriant, spontaneous thrust of nature. The translation into Greek would be physical autonomy. In *The Theaetetus*, Plato wrote: that is free which follows its own law (*auto-nomos*). What it is to be free for the budding plant is to manage to arrive at the flowering stage. For human beings, to leave neotenic, pedagogic and, lastly, political dependence behind and succeed in acceding to solitude—this is the *imago* of the human being. For *phusis*, the *imago* designates the state in which an individual finds itself at the end of its metamorphoses. A being's liberty is not opposed to the determinations of *phusis* but stands opposed to social life, its orders, its domestic space and its chains. Liberty rounds off human *phusis*, whereas slavery (wage labour, religious ritual, forbidden suicide) constrains the body and subdues the soul to the point of inhibition. It was not only nature that the Greeks termed *phusis* but also the male sex organ. We may combine, then, Aristotle's phrase 'Liberty is *phusis*' with Melanie Klein's 'Solitude is the programme.' This gives us the argument that the fulfilment of the destiny of a human being is freedom of the self, conceived as the ability to live alone.

In this way, the etymology of the Greek *eleutheros* (*to elthein opou erâ*) connects with that of the French word *sauvage* (wild or savage).

French *sauvage* breaks down into Latin *soli-vagus*—he who wanders solitarily.

What is liberty? It is what sounds the call back to originary wildness. For little children were like cats. Theirs is a wildness which, being once domesticated, leaves behind a nostalgia in every child whom involuntary obedience within the family and the voluntary servitude of education have driven first into admiration, then into childhood training and, lastly, into the shame of slavery.

Such is *feritas* in Latin, the state of the wild beast, which in French is the origin of the word *fierté* (pride), in the same way as the *soli-vagari* of felines, wild boars and stags gives French the word *sauvagerie*—wildness.

*

Human freedom connects with this disaffection on the part of solitaries—itself an animal affair—with hordes or packs.

*

A nameless drive, originating nowhere, motiveless and preference-less, tenses, advances, wanders. *Solus vagari in agris, errore vagari*—to ramble about aimlessly hither and yon, to climb trees, scale rocks, roam about the fields. To forget home, family, childhood and dependency. This wandering or straying (Latin: *error*) is what the chivalric 'forest of adventure' was about. These are the solitary rambles over the moors that Emily Bronte loved more than anything in the world. Pliny (V, 31) speaks of *vagantes fabulae*, of contradictory, wild, erratic, drifting stories. This is the king's life that I lead in the last of kingdoms.

CHAPTER 32

The Definition of 'The Open'

Socrates the Athenian shows his pleasure at release into the 'open' at the beginning of the *Phaedo*, when the guard comes and removes his irons: he rubs his benumbed ankles.

Socrates is going to die but that matters little: he finds pleasure in rubbing his battered, bare legs, from which the irons have just been removed.

*

Writing novels removes irons. Novels imagine another life. These images and journeys gradually lead to situations which, in the life of the reader, as in the life of the writer, free us from the habits of life.

*

What is another life but another linguistic plot?
Open space does exist.

*

Writing destroys the compulsion within the soul to
repeat the past.

What is the point of writing? To avoid a living
death.

*

Open space has found a place for itself everywhere on
this earth. In books. Reading frees one to roam the
open spaces.

*

Who will give me back my Italian life, my free life?
The life in which I could go anywhere? Always out,

always outside reading or dreaming? Living beneath
the boughs of the trees or the shade of parasols?

CHAPTER 33

Autarkès

The key element for the freest of human beings is not their clothing, their home, their identity card, their obituary, their car, their fire insurance or their coupledom. The element in which their fervour, their desire, their licence, their spontaneity, their familiarity and their boldness most readily develop is their body. It is the solitude of desiring nakedness; waking at dead of night, one's body dripping with sweat; coming out of a dream. At that point something of oneself is experienced physically. In that sudden awakening of the body an extremely rapid 'physico-psychical self-recognition' takes place. I am not going to stray far from the ancient shore of the Greeks. I shall follow Epicurus' Greek step by step. Against social *paideia*, writes Epicurus, we must set a *physiologia*. The function of that physiology is to exercise the 'body's eros' to the point of sensual delight. Only this—almost gymnastic, but in no way political, and in many of its features downright anti-social—*physiologia* is capable of producing animals that are not neutered, that are full of life, not docile, striving to be lucid, free of veils, tributes, functions, heritages, symbols, coins, linguistic functors and tragic masks. They are, word for word, 'proud', 'independent' men or, alternatively, 'men who pride themselves on what is their own'. Epicurus at this point uses the Greek epithets *sobaroi* and *autarkeis*.

The Greek word *autarkès* that he uses is the Latin *ferus*.

First molecule: the French word *fier*, ferocious animal, independent man, naked desire.

Second molecule, a little more complex: *autarkès ferus hager solivagus*—alone wandering proud. I am a man always mildly amazed, a little scared, silent, shy, worried—haggard. 'Haggard' comes from *hagger*, a Middle English word that corresponds to the Latin *ferus* and refers to wild or untamed animals. If the Latin *soli-vagus* translates word for word as wandering alone, the English word *hagger* denotes the untameable, as well as the uncultivable. The falcon is said to be 'haggard' when the hood by which it was blinded is removed and it suddenly sees, flies off and hunts once again. *Ferox* refers to a spirit that cannot be tamed. It must be remembered that all pride—*fierté*—is, as a consequence, (1) *ferox* and (2) *hager*. It was hunting that carried humanity to play. Hunting was the most concentrated bloody game known to humanity, before human beings developed war out of it. War is the hunt in which the beast hunted is one's fellow creature. For its part, hunting refers to *imitated* animal predation. Hunting disjoined men from collective obedience—that is to say, obedience to their families, their mothers, their elders. In a necessarily centrifugal movement, hunters went to the periphery of groups, ventured into distant spaces. The home was where old people, women, children, fire, resources and the granary were gathered and settled. If Latin *pangere* means to 'fix' a place in space, this 'fixed place' in Latin groups together *pagus* (French *pays*), page and peace. Imitating predation forced those who hunted into what was not the *pagus* (district or locality), into an area that was not 'peace', into the *limes*; they were forced to lie in wait, to keep still, to dissimulate, to be silent. In this way, hunters came to keep a distance, then to be separated—first by withdrawal into silence, then into secrecy—from the homestead, from reproduction, from women (from fertility, the genealogical secret, the mystery of their menstruation and from the confluence of immediate resources and sedentary properties). Hunters compared themselves with the other animals they stalked. They became psychologized. Journeys are memorized individually. Returns—great there-and-back journeys, great ecliptic circles—exist only for the hunters on land and sea. The Greek word for return is *nostos*, which creates both the individual journey and a sense of location. The hunting story is individual (even if the homestead is the goal of one's return, just as the narrative that completes that return is aimed at the mother, sole mistress of the renewal of the social).

Most men tend to be examples of humanity integrated into the general species.

A non-exemplary, non-reproducible movement out beyond the family and society, is extremely rare.

Unheroic indisciplinarity is difficult.

°It is the *secessio plebis*.

*

The story of the emergence within a national collectivity of a free individual, or one who is at least more or less autonomous, belongs to the realm of adventure narratives. Arthur Schnitzler wrote a fine autobiographical work, the French translation of which was curiously entitled *Vienne au crépuscule* (Vienna at Twilight). The title Schnitzler gave to his book in 1905 was far from evoking the beginnings of a night that has not yet fallen. °It was *Der Weg ins Freie*. The title of the French translation of Schnitzler's book is not just anachronistic but mendacious. There is a joy in finding oneself alone again. The plot of the book is strange—very limited and anxiety-ridden. A woman wants to bear a child and to do so as a married woman. All through the book, the man who loves her is constantly running away. He refuses to conceive of love as the possession of reproduction in honour of the group. Schnitzler, torn between two courses of action, writes that he ends up 'alone, a little proud of that solitude, a little troubled by that pride'.

*

Epicurus wrote that the *sophos* (sage) would have no concern for his tomb; would deny the gods; would not engage in politics; would not get drunk; would not depend on anyone; would not marry. He would contemplate Nature and sexual pleasure would be his end, as it had been the source of his days.

CHAPTER 34

Menephron

Menephron never saw a stretch of calm water. He never saw a surface of bronze. His whole life long he knew nothing of his face.

Freedom begins in the absence of a face.

CHAPTER 35

Dogs obey the one who dominates them. They are pack animals, passionate for integration; they love rewards and adore leaders. The attachment of dogs to their masters is so incredible as to have become legendary. This faithfulness has astonished humanity. Admittedly, all the tales that tell of it, whether they refer to wolves or to wolves when they have become dogs, are fairy tales.

I used to love cats. In their eyes, relations of subordination do not exist. Dependency is their enemy. Only territory is god. Freedom is their only value. Licking and stroking, eating, hunting, playing at hunting, dreaming of hunting or just dreaming and dreaming again are sufficient to fill their days.

Suddenly they raise their heads and lap the fresh air swirling like water round their tiny noses.

CHAPTER 36

°Étienne de La Boétie wrote: 'Even the beasts cry "Long live liberty!" There are several among them that die as soon as they are taken.' Naevius names Bacchus *Liber, id est pro libertas*—free god because he is liberty made god. For the citizens of the United States of America, liberty is a statue in the middle of a port that gives direction to shipping, that serves as a customs post, that repels foreigners. It is possible that a country in which you are permitted not to love the gods, to smoke tobacco while waiting for a train, to drink wine on a cafe terrace in the street, to walk round without identity papers and everywhere to say what you believe, no longer exists in this world.

°At the end of the Second World War, to those who sought asylum there, the Canadians replied: 'No one!' Not one, not a single one.

'Not a single free man!' is the watchword of the social.

Hunting animals, angling for fish, drinking water, lying where the sun shines, following river banks and wandering along beaches have all become impossible to do without money in the course of my lifetime and before my very eyes.

It is true that liberty has its attendant sadness which we must not try to conceal.

The sadness of the farewell to what had thus far held you prisoner. This sadness is of the order of widowhood. The sense of guilt liberty generates is never entirely extinguished. Even if you have had every reason in the world to leave your own people, you remain one of them.

What course of action is indicated? To stay alive, in good physical condition, half-awake, half-asleep, half-excited, half-sad, half-animal, half-human, half-myself, half-nobody.

We must take cats as an example, as they pad cautiously along the guttering. We must watch how they arch their backs before leaping to reach the next roof.

Half-bold, half-fearful. This caution is all the politics in the world.

*

Epictetus wrote: 'Fear of the scarers makes the stags run into the nets, where they perish.' Because he was a slave, and because he was the slave of a slave, Epictetus is the thinker who found the greatest number of definitions for the word liberty.

He is free whom one cannot constrain.

He is free whose wrists are not shackled.

He is free who is not hungry and is without desire.

He is free who is not a slave (the animal is free that is not tamed).

He is free who takes advantage of the door that has been left open (he who commits suicide is free).

He is free who does not ask permission from anyone.

He is free who does not defer to any authority.

Every man is a citadel full of tyrants that have to be driven out.

Say each day, as you exercise your body in muscle-building exercises, before offering it up for massage, and as you exercise your mind in thought, before offering it up to dreams:

'No, not apprentice philosopher but slave in process of emancipation!'

*

Addictus in Latin referred to someone enslaved for debt. To be 'emancipated' means to be 'without addiction'.

CHAPTER 37

Kronstadt was the name of the Russian fleet's Baltic naval base, nestling on the island of Kotlin, which protected Saint Petersburg.

In 1905 the mutinies began. After that, they never ended. Kronstadt is insurrectional liberty as island. All the sailors were exterminated. No one— not one of them—survived. Kronstadt is the island *par excellence*. The *ipsima* island.

*

Two lands loved books. They are still islands. The civilized world is polarized by two nations at the two ends of the planet. They are the finest of islands, the most extreme of islands, Japan and Iceland.

*

A few fragments of earth lost at sea, a few individuals in the towns, a few bookish people in their rooms, a few atheists, a few scholars, a few anchorites. These islands, these caves, these cephalic cavities, these rooms, these hermitages are the last of kingdoms. Rare are the beings that enjoy a little of the island in their souls by virtue of the void that lies beneath their hands. Thoughts that stray from the norm are very scarce in the depths of the mind, so much is the soul peopled by family, language, education, addiction, past, memory, repetition, instinct and nature. '*Rara*,' said Spinoza, referring to this inner experience of liberty.

What most gives us the sense of liberty? *Forgetting that you are being watched.*

No longer being either a child or an old person, neither a woman nor a man, neither a father nor a mother, neither a son nor a daughter.

There is no—collective—looking over their shoulders.

They know no domestication in the emotions of their voices. Forget the realms to which language consigns us. Our corporeal depths hold neither the cultivated nor the tamed, neither society nor language. In springtime the new heat of the sun frees the drift ice. This is the break-up of the ice floes. Freedom is a break-up of the ice.

CHAPTER 38

Marvellous Hatred

After the Greek Athenion had led a slave revolt, the Servile Wars left rows of thousands of crosses along the roads of Northern Italy. The victims howled like the dogs lingering round their feet, wishing for flesh to fall so as to underscore their faithful natures by making it their own. The seagulls, crows, vultures and owls flew above the faces of the rebel slaves who had been crucified. Everywhere death was visible. Everywhere there was a stench of suffering, dead flesh. It spurred on the bodies of the citizens to kill even more. Yet when Vernatus the aedile learnt of the death of Gaius Hiero, who was Athenion's protector, he wept. Before becoming a Roman aedile, Vernatus had fought against Hiero during the Second Civil War. Since the whole of the city of Rome knew how much Vernatus hated Hiero, his intimates, his relatives, his friends and clients thought the announcement of Hiero's death would bring him pleasure. They went, all in a crowd, to find him at the port, where Vernatus was busy overseeing the unloading of one of his galleys. They found him. They acclaimed him. They said: 'Vernatus, rejoice. Your enemy is dead.'

But to everyone's surprise, Vernatus wept.

He sat down on a bale of flower petals that was waiting to be taken to the perfumer's and wept.

Then the aedile pressed back his tears and announced to the men round him: 'You see me unhappy because I have not been the cause of my enemy's death. I had vengeance to exact and what have I done? Nothing. I stayed here twiddling my thumbs and sitting on a bale of flowers.'

'It's chance.'

'He was young.'

'You were young.'

'It's good fortune.'

'It's luck.'

'No,' said Vernatus. 'I was a man at the port watching the ships go by, watching them come in, watching them being unloaded.'

This was, indeed, the truth. He was a man sitting on a bale on the quayside, watching one of his galleys being unloaded. In the evening when he went home, he told his wife: 'You will prepare my luggage tomorrow and put it alongside my weapons.'

'What need do you have of your weapons?'

'What does it matter to you?'

Since his wife was suspicious, she repeated her question: 'What need do you have of your weapons, Vernatus?'

Vernatus struck her with such violence that she fell to the ground.

'Forgive me,' she said, as she tried to get up. He did not help her up. He said:

'I have nothing to forgive you for. I am going away. Tomorrow I shall arm myself with the weapons you have prepared. I shall take my chestnut horse.'

As his wife gazed at him sadly, he added: 'Go and do what I asked you to.'

The aedile's wife, assisted by the servants, did what he had asked.

While she was preparing his luggage and his weapons, Vernatus went to find his eldest son and told him: 'I fought once with a horseman in the Appenines. Another time, I did so in the Valley of the Tevere.'

'I take it you are speaking of Hiero.'

'It is of him that I speak. I am going to go and pay tribute to him before I die.'

'But, father, you have just learnt that he is dead!'

'I shall say again, I am going to go and pay tribute to him because I feel age catching up with me, particularly at the top of my shoulders.'

'Right.'

'Son, I am now entrusting the house, its staff, your mother, the animals, all the crops and all the vessels to your care.'

'Since you say so.'

The next day, by the time everyone was up Vernatus had gone. He left his house the same way Camillus had left Rome when accused by Lucius Apuleius, except that Vernatus refrained from threats. He was accompanied only by a manservant and an enormous hound. All five of them (the aedile, the horse, the dog, the manservant and the mule) went to Umbria. Vernatus the aedile enquired among the local people. They pointed out to him where the body of Gaius Hiero was buried. A grave had been dug beneath an umbrella pine on top of a hill west of Spoleto. To a horseman who asked him why he was looking for a man he disliked and who had been deceased for some days, he said: 'I liked having the man as my enemy.'

*

Vernatus came out of the forest. He finally reached the valley. He saw a little winding river in front of him. Above it, he saw a settlement of ten or fifteen houses surrounded by blue hills.

As the hills came closer, they grew whiter and whiter.

They lost none of their beauty in coming closer and growing whiter but they turned themselves into a kind of vapour. At the time he arrived, with the sun in the west and not yet twilight, the solar light struck the contours of the hill laterally. He could see the sun's rays pouring down from the clouds like shafts of light. He saw them falling on the roof of one of the largest farms, illuminating the doorposts of the stables and the crossbeams of the barns. He also saw the light agglutinating into little drops on tiny herds—on cows, calves, sheep, the dogs that protected them, and an umbrella pine. For all these things seemed as tiny as grain before it is crushed beneath the millstone and the heavy light, the very heavy light of the sun coming out of the cloud heaped itself on them. Tiny as they were, white and sometimes pink, dotted upon the gold of the meadow, the sun's gleam lit up each one. Vernatus pointed with his hand to the umbrella pine that rose up in the mist, spreading its black foliage into it, and said to his companion: 'I have known some stunning moments. The place where Gaius Hiero wanted to be buried is, indeed, a very pleasant hill. But the most stunning experience the soul can know comes not from beauty but from hatred. The wild beasts do not give that a name but they live it out in their silence. The desire to kill that fires them, or melts them, or prompts them to leap on their prey, or incites them to pounce, is more beautiful than beauty and older than Romulus himself. Moreover, Romulus felt it suddenly towards Remus when he laid him out in the ditch. Hatred is truly a marvellous feeling.'

*

Night fell. Vernatus dismounted. He handed over the reins of his horse to the tavern keeper. His buttocks were dripping with sweat. He washed them, for they burnt him. He refused to go into the main hall. He did not eat but sat drinking sour white wine on the atrium bench. In the presence of the innkeeper he recounted his life story. His faithful dog, wearied by the journey and knowing his master's life story by heart, slept and snored at his feet. What had his life been? Wars to the death. What were the joys of wars to the death? There, once again, it was the manifestations of hatred. In war the blood flooded the whole body even more than when sexual desire pumped through it and made it erect. One's eyes were all undivided attention. Addressing himself to the tavernkeeper, Vernatus the aedile concluded:

'When I learnt of the natural death of the one who had been the target of my thoughts for so many years, I felt in the depths of my body something leave me so suddenly that I had to sit down on a bale of flowers.'

'Ah,' said the tavernkeeper. 'The gods were with you! Lucky there was a bale there!'

These were their only words. The tavernkeeper and the manservant slept. Vernatus did not. When the first gleams of light appeared in the night sky, he left his bench, spat, pissed, took his weapon and went out. He went down the little alleyway. At length he came to the path leading to the hillside. Dawn was gradually tinting the dark sky. There were no clouds. He walked in the growing light that spread itself gently above the black hills, whose curves were visible on the far horizon. As it rose, little by little the sun plunged the settlement into shadow. The only thing to be seen with precision was a farm on the hillside, sheathed entirely in white light. The animals had not yet come out of their sheds. His manservant had stayed behind, sleeping in the inn. Vernatus had left his horse in the stable in the courtyard behind the tavern. He walked his final path alone. Only his faithful, yelping dog played about his feet and among the stones. At a certain point, when he ran into the cool breeze blowing along the riverbank, he chose suddenly to follow it.

*

Vernatus climbed the fourth hill. It was covered with vines. The umbrella pine stood to the east and he headed for it. He made out a little tumulus and walked towards it. The incipient pink sun rose directly in his face, so that he had to screw up his eyelids and blink his eyes to read the gravestone. On it he could make out the homage that had been paid 'by the second citizen of the town of Spoleto to the first among his people'. He placed his hand on the stone. He laid his metal helmet down on the grass of the burial mound. He placed his leather-covered shield (*scutum*) against the stone. He lay down slowly, by first bending his legs. Then he dropped down heavily on to the ground. Next he bent his elbow and allowed his bulky body to slump on to its side, exactly as the African lion does when it has time to rest in the sand. With his face still in full sunlight and his head still rising stiffly from his shoulders, his eyes took in the pleasant hills around him.

*

A little later the faithful hound came and curled up against his sex and his knees. An hour before midday, the manservant joined them. He was holding the reins of the horse and the mule, but the aedile made no movement, not even of the head, towards the mounts when they approached. At midday, when the sun's rays fell vertically on his head of hair, he took the double-edged sword from his scabbard and brought it up to his heart. The manservant, the horse, the mule, the shepherds and also the string of little girls watching from a distance thought he was going to plunge it into his breast. But he did not. He planted it in the mound that covered the body of Hiero. He plunged the sword into the earth up to the hilt, no doubt touching his enemy's body, doing so as though he hoped to pierce his heart. Vernatus stayed there, lying in the dust of the mound, his hand on the hilt of the sword, not changing his position, urinating several times beneath himself, remaining alongside his own ordure, starving himself to death. It took a fortnight for him to die, in contact with his enemy, but Vernatus' body remained on the mound for twenty-six days. The local inhabitants did not know what was to be done with this corpse that threatened to defile their fields. They feared its presence, its smell, its rottenness, its morbidity would compromise their harvests. Vernatus' manservant therefore went to Spoleto. He put the question to the tribunal but the magistrates of the city of Spoleto did not know how to answer. The birds pecked away at the body. The dog gnawed at his master's remains, howling. An eagle, suddenly poking its head into one of the dead man's eye sockets, dislodged his brain and managed to extract it, sucking at its marvellous hatred. All kinds of birds circled the tomb in all directions, devouring whatever they managed to snap up or tear from the body. The inhabitants of the province said it was the shades of the two dead men that had called their friends and clients to their aid and were fighting it out between them.

CHAPTER 39

Vernatus is the bringer of birds. *Ver* to the Romans meant spring.

I would suggest that the first experience of the finite is not human death.

It is not even the preparation of dead animals each day—three times a day—to feed oneself.

The first experience of finitude is winter.

In winter, before human beings did so, pregnant she-bears made their way into caves. The spring was hiding. The return of young was redeveloping within wombs. A world in motion breaks through on the cave wall, lit by the first pinewood torch brandished by the hand of a man fearful of a cold, hungry death.

*

In Latin, the human mouth designates winter. Varro wrote: '*Ab hiatu hiems*': the opening of the mouth in winter says 'winter' by dint of the white vapour into which one's breath and words are immediately transformed, sacrificing tenor and meaning, acceding directly to the originary status of animal breath being breathed out and falling before our eyes.

Death is hungry in the mouth of winter.

Death is the *famished one* deep within us. Before anthropomorphosis, before the representation of Hell, it stakes its claim, opening the aoristic maw by which it has been represented since the days of the fascinating great wild beasts.

CHAPTER 40

The Prague city clock on the main square. When it sounds the hours, the Turk with his mandolin, the rich man with his purse of silver and Vanity with his mirror—all three shake their heads to say 'no' to Death which, silently opening its mouth, replies 'yes.'

CHAPTER 41

ºBossuet's Mouth

When he became Bishop of Meaux, Monseigneur Allou set people searching for the tomb of the most illustrious of his predecessors. It was found. The coffin was exhumed from the sanctuary. It was opened on 14 November 1854. The vicar-general of the diocese—Abbot Josse by name—drafted the official account of the condition in which Doctor Houzelot found Bossuet's head, after the lead had been loosened over a length of five feet ten inches. Monseigneur Allou then asked Monsieur Maillot, who was a painter, to 'sketch the face of Bénigne Bossuet, author of the *Universal History*, extricated from the shrouds in which it was enwrapped'. The vicar-general noted: 'Being moved by his subject and with his drawing to make, the Painter's pencil trembled in his fingers.' Subsequently, the lithographer

Edmond Morin reproduced the sketch that Charles Maillot had made. Abbot Josse compared subject, sketch and engraving. He wrote: 'The mouth is wide open, the tongue withered, the eyes entirely destroyed. Their dust has mingled with the remains of the eyelids and fills the orbital cavities. Monsieur Maillot's drawing, more than Monsieur Morin's lithograph, reinforces this frightful impression, showing the mouth, once so eloquent, gaping wide in death towards the Hereafter.

CHAPTER 42

Approaching death is in no sense a thing to flee from, as the absurd, tonic, positive, religious morality of the moderns maintains. Death has its season, which is no more irksome than the others. When the season of death is here—what everyone calls winter—it so happens that the sky reverts to an intense blue.

The earth crunches beneath our feet.

The pond is never so clean as when it is frozen.

The leaves have disappeared.

Flowers, birds, people and names—everything has disappeared.

It is so clear.

*

If we had never experienced winter, we shouldn't have found death an easily accessible notion.

Winter so spells death for us that we needed to see winter itself die.

The god Winter was put to death every year at the end of three months of darkness and hunger.

Bacchus is a *Januarius*.

In Rome, the god known in Greek as Dionysos Nyktipolos was called the 'Bacchus who wanders in the long winter night'. Dadophorios, God of torches and caves. The Nocturnal Hunter transforms himself into the headless, tailless horse that throws to the ground the one who tries to mount him. In this way he turns against himself. He becomes the hunter hunted. The render rent. Dionysus Anthroporraistès means Bacchus Render of Men, and Zagreus is glossed as *o megalos agreuôn*, the Great Hunter. He is the prey who is also predator.

An eater of raw meat, *ômèstès*, the dog Cerberus licks the feet or hoofs of this Zagreus, son of Hades.

All the wolves and dogs come to greet this Saint Nicholas with his club and flaxen beard as though he were their master.

Bacchus is the guardian of the Underworld, who is killed at the end of winter. The old year dies in him. He is torn apart while yet alive and reborn as a child.

In this way death extended a new limit—each year anew—at the close of each reborn year, within the natural space of the terrestrial human presence.

The limit of human time became the year.

Later, time in the West was conceived as an end.

Yet, for whoever meditates on this vast world, so much more immense than beings, time is much more temporal—more swaggering—in its original modality. It is the starting point: springtime against a backdrop of winter. It is the fact of beginning, then emerging by birth into the world; falling in a secondary way into the second world, which bites as the cold bites, which bites like a hungry man gripping something desperately between his teeth. This time seeks living death. In the *primum tempus* of the *printemps* (spring), it is the beginning that enwraps us with finitude, that bowls us over with finitude, that at times induces us to lay hold of the end so as to be finished.

*

One forces oneself to turn one's head towards the face of that which will not rise again. These wide open eyes no longer have sight for us. This mouth no longer gives an answer. Death is the departure of movement, of expressions, of language, of sight.

Every caress is extinguished.

Pure departure without return, as is birth with its cry.

Pure leaving, like sensual delight in its strange moaning.

Another's death carries on something from our birth, which meant suddenly being frustrated of the body in which we were located.

Another time—which stands for every other time—our body stands before an earlier body which now becomes unknown.

*

Death is like language. Death is a machine for obliterating conditions of appearance. Death, like language, brings the unseeable with it. More than this, it brings with it the *unforeseeable*. Matthew 25:13 says *Nescitis diem neque horam*. 'Ye know neither the day nor the hour.' The definition of death is pure time. Man, in the depths of the one who speaks, is merely time responding to language.

*

The nuptials took place, since our body is here. The door of the room has closed again. He said: *Nescio vos*. 'I know you not.' He said: *Vigilitate itaque qui nescitis diem, neque horam.* 'Watch therefore, for ye know neither the day nor the hour.'

Watch, for it is not perhaps from the death which threatens our bodies and our days that questioning arises.

The first 'why' (Latin: *cur*) is born of the visionless unknown which is our genesis so far as the soul is concerned.

From the outset, diachrony forces us to ally with the unknown in the form of the never-visible.

Will it be in winter? Will it be in summer?

Will it be in the town? In the country? In the forest? On the riverbank?

Will it be in the middle of the day? In the street? Stretched out on the roadway or on the pavement? In front of everyone? Will it be after nightfall? In one's bed? Out of sight?

Will it be from suffering? Or sickness? Accident? Exhaustion? Will it be during a dream? Will it be at the moment of desire?

CHAPTER 43

At Candlemas the priest is called upon in the Communion service to bless candles. These are lit each time a storm rages overhead. These are the candles that are put at the bedside of the dying. We need temporal aids when time is being rent asunder.

CHAPTER 44

On the eve of his assassination, as Caesar was dining at the house of Marcus Lepidus, the guests happened to discuss the most desirable kind of death.

Caesar, lifting his face from his plate, said: *Repentinum et inopinatum.* Very quick and entirely unexpected.

The emperor Marcus Aurelius takes a different view from Caesar the dictator. °In his *Towards Myself,* Marcus Aurelius wrote in Greek: Death is like the appearance of the teeth; it is like the growing of the beard; it is like the ejaculation of sperm. Life is a metamorphosis that has one of its points of repose in death, as it has another in orgasm, another in the constitution of the jaw, as seen in skeletons, another in sleep. It is in this way that death calls down death on the survivor, who will be consumed by his memory.

CHAPTER 45

Tulips, mosquitos, elephants, storms over land, may-flies, ladybirds, daisies, whales, mountains and sea storms appear, rise, grow, suddenly repeat their forms, their bodies, their fates and disappear.

Flowers rise up, ejaculate, fall.

For flowers, death is called apoptosis.

It is simply a matter of falling.

Where better in time to lodge unforeseeability than in death?

In the furtiveness of personal death, so far as its date is concerned, a strange companionship is estab-lished. Here death, like time, adds the irrevocable to the unforeseeable.

In the word irrevocable we should stress the uninvocable quality that defines the human status of corpses: it is a body that no longer responds to the words one pleadingly addresses to it.

What is a dead man for human beings? Someone who no longer takes part in the dialogue.

The mouth that no longer responds to language.

Within the unforeseeable, the irrevocable defines the 'surprise of silence' on the face.

*

It is surprise and asynchrony, which are the specific features of death, that stand frontally opposed to repetition and history.

Birth stands over against childhood as irruption does against repetition.

As silence stands over against addiction to language.

New, entire, intact, virgin, first, novice, *rising* sun, greenness, freshness, youth, youthfulness stand over against *repetitio, renovatio, revolutio*. Present, modern, contemporary refer to one and the same rehashing of the past. The young re-new.

The 'new-style', which is the opposite of the young, innovates (it does not renew; it rejuvenates nothing).

The new does not repeat, it *invents*.

*

Nature becomes once again matter that overflows through this temporal door that death opens in the site where it suddenly spaces out space by decomposing bodily forms in death.

This space opened by death, which extends its *posse* into the heart of the *esse*, is time.

*

A century ago, Darwin assigned death a function. Death selected how nature would be animated, like a predator cleaning up the marks of origin. Death was like a priest who polished the golden statue of the god in the temple. Having been an agent of differentiation, death now became a rejuvenator. In human societies the maintenance of the world would have a cost for all the living organisms that peopled the earth. That price was death.

The head of the old man is gradually transformed into the head of an infant.

The ribcage remains in the state of expiration.

The eyes are still open.

But the corpse has not yet 'passed on'. Life within the dead body is not over. You have to wait patiently for at least a year for the flesh to decompose.

After five years, the flesh having decomposed, the bones fall apart.

This is what the time of death is like. The component elements deprogramme themselves and reunite with the common fund that constitutes life.

The oceans organize two major forms of the recycling of dead organisms: consumption on the surface, re-mineralization in the depths.

The teeth form the most immortal part of human bodies.

This is no doubt what Marcus Aurelius meant when he wrote 'Death is like the appearance of the teeth.'

This explains the invention of inhumation among humans. If to bury is to snatch from being devoured, then it is to prefer organic decomposition to claws, beaks and teeth.

Thus all larger living animals, when faced with the dead, are morsels of time fearful of the teeth that lie in wait for all that lives and, hence, can be devoured.

*

°In the *Nekuomanteia*, Lucian writes: 'We went down into the Underworld. We entered the Acherusian plain and there found the demigods, the great hunters, the heroines, the queens. The ancient Achaeans were decayed and mouldy. The Egyptians solid and embalmed. But we recognized no one. They were all absolutely alike; no other signs were discernible except *protruding teeth*.'

CHAPTER 46

The caterpillar knows nothing of the butterfly whose metamorphic cocoon it constructs.

The spider spins its predatory web without knowing its prey.

Music does the same with its song.

And language with its book.

CHAPTER 47

The Singing Festivals of the Marais

In the sixteenth century, in the Marais quarter in Paris, there was, each year at the end of March, a highly esteemed singing competition for children. All who appreciated the singing of small boys with unbroken voices attended in order to make their choice and purchase the best for their choirs. In 1581, Bernon, nicknamed 'The Child'—he was nine years old at the time—was the main attraction. Yet he did not win the prize, since he was a Protestant. In 1582 he was not entered by his choir school and Marcellin from Palaiseau, a very handsome child, was declared the winner. In 1583 it happened that Bernon the Child surpassed his competitors with such virtuosity that the crowd demanded an encore from him. He sang another song and triumphed.

The previous year's winner, who was called Marcellin, was relegated to fifth place.

Marcellin, nicknamed 'le Palaiseau' or 'le beau Palaiseau' was a Catholic. He was all of twelve years of age and sang at the chantry of the basilica of Palaiseau, a village situated near Paris. He already had fears that his voice might be about to break. He thought, 'Bernon had already sung once. By singing a second time, he took the place of another choir school that should have been presented after him. We were not given equal chances.' Marcellin looked out for Bernon as they were leaving the Marais. He drew him aside. He took him by the arm and said: 'Last year I was the winner. Come with me. There's something it's customary for the winners to see. I'll show it to you. Follow me.'

Bernon followed him without hesitation. Marcellin drew him to the bottom of the slope that leads down to the Seine. Once the two children were hidden by rushes, le Palaiseau ran The Child through with a knife. He cut off his head, peeled the skin from his face and made him unrecognizable. °He threw his body into the waters of the Seine that flow towards the port of Le Havre de Grâce. He hid the utterly dis-figured face beneath the rocks on the bank.

*

A year passed.

The Marais singing festival came round again.

Le beau Palaiseau betook himself to it. Just as he was crossing the bridge that leads from the Ile de la Cité to the area known as the Strand, he heard in the distance a voice singing wondrously on the riverbank. He looked all around him. There was no one there. Unsettled by this, le Palaiseau walked down to the bank. He went, of his own accord, towards the clump of bulrushes at the river's edge. There was a large black boat there, which was empty and floating gently on the dark water. The invisible voice sang the fol-lowing lines:

'As long as I am lost, my soul will go on singing. My name has not rejoined my body, which has gone down to the sea. I am not dead, but disappeared.'

Le Palaiseau leant over, pushed aside the black boat, lifted up the stones at the bottom of the bank and looked beneath the moss. There he came upon the whitened skull of Bernon the Child, which was singing. He touched it, it stopped singing. The fish and the spiders had completely stripped it of its flesh. Le Palaiseau took away the skull under his cloak. Within the palisades of the city, he presented himself for the singing tournament. Not only did the Catholic singer not win the children's competition in the Marais but he was hooted down, since approaching puberty had begun to ruin his voice.

*

Time passed.

The spring passed.

One summer's day, le Palaiseau travelled to a Protestant-held town on the road leading to the sea: he went into an inn. He took out the little skull from under his cloak. He scored a great success by letting the wondrous death's head sing. For weeks and weeks le Palaiseau went from inn to inn. All the men and women who listened were torn between terror and emotion. He amassed a great deal of money. The rumour of his exploits grew. It reached the ears of the governor of the port of La Rochelle. The governor would not believe what he was being told. He got off his horse and said to Thonon the Innkeeper:

'This is Catholic propaganda. I don't believe you. I've never seen skulls sing.'

'This skull sings,' maintained Thonon, 'and I can't be suspected of being a Catholic!'

The governor lost his temper and said, 'If it were truly the case that a skull were able to sing, I'd pay the little mountebank showing it off everywhere his weight in gold.'

This promise did not fall on deaf ears. Le beau Palaiseau immediately went to La Rochelle. He was radiant with joy. He was like a sun. He beamed with arrogance and seemed all the more handsome as a result. He ate constantly for three days. Looking hale and hearty, he entered the palace. The governor asked him if he belonged to the Catholic League:

'Yes.'

'We have little fondness for it.'

'I know.'

'Why are you here?'

'I am taking the singing skull from town to town.'

'What is your name?'

'Marcellin.'

'Where are you from?'

'My parents live in the damp valley of Palaiseau.'

'What do you do?'

'I was a chorister in the basilica but my voice broke and the chapter of canons dismissed me.'

'Precisely what profession do you follow now?'

'Now I go from town to town displaying the singing skull.'

'Be careful, Marcellin. I detest liars as much as I hate Catholics.'

'I know.'

The governor said: 'Either this skull sings and you'll be showered with gold. Or you'll be as dead as that skull you conceal beneath your cloak.'

Le beau Palaiseau smiled, sure of himself. He said: 'Personally, your Excellency, I would like you to weigh me first.'

The governor replied curtly, 'Do you doubt the word of the Captain of the Port? Do you suspect the word of a Protestant?'

'Not at all! I don't doubt you! I suspect nothing! But it would give me pleasure to see what my weight in gold looks like. You promised Thonon the Innkeeper. I've done nothing but eat for three days.'

The governor of La Rochelle regarded Thonon the Innkeeper who was in the room. They brought a butcher's scales. The handsome adolescent stripped naked. They looked him up and down. He was a Catholic and hence loved to be admired. They weighed him. Once weighed, beaming, le beau Palaiseau gazed at the pile of gold they had heaped up in front of him. He dressed again, taking great care over it; he took the skull out from under his cloak; he placed it delicately on the heap of gold the governor of the port of La Rochelle had counted out for him, which stood there in front of everyone.

All then fell silent.

Le Palaiseau turned to the skull and bade it sing.

The skull did not sing.

Despite le Palaiseau's words and threats, the skull did not sing.

Le Palaiseau went very pale.

'You lied,' said the governor.

'Sing!' screamed le beau Paliseau.

No song came.

The captain signalled to his men. The man closest to le Palaiseau took a long dagger from its leather scabbard and cut down the adolescent with a few well-directed blows. Blood spurted from each of his wounds. All this blood flowed out and gathered. The rivulet of blood ran to the feet of the governor, reaching up to his spurs.

At that same moment, on its silk cushion—and with a marvellously pure voice—the skull began to sing.

The skull had chosen the song entitled 'Joy of Vengeance'.

The governor of the port of La Rochelle could not believe his ears.

A musician who happened to be there said, 'That's the voice of Bernon the Child. I heard it in 1581 at the competition held in the Marais in Paris.'

The governor of the port of La Rochelle was enchanted, in the proper sense of the word. He listened to the skull not only for the rest of the day but the whole night through. However, as the days passed, he and his entourage grew weary. 'Joy of Vengeance' was the only song the skull knew. They took the skull up to the Grenier des Réformés and abandoned it there to the dust.

CHAPTER 48

When Gorky discovered the cinema, he immediately named it the Kingdom of the Shadows. It was 4 July 1896. Gorky wrote: 'I am not speaking of a living world. I am speaking of a colourless world that knows no sound. I am not speaking of life but of the shadow of life. Something comes out of the background and rushes towards your eyes. It is terrifying to see, this movement of shadows coming towards you at great speed from the depths of the picture. This violent projection of ghosts repeating their gestures for eternity is like a nightmare from which you never entirely manage to awake. What I saw left me soaked in sweat. A distant nighttime scene emerges, comes towards us, swallows us up and then disappears into silence.'

*

Words hover on the tip of the tongue, where, not being natives of the place, they are unfindable.

Desynchrony is the regime of the *Vivipara*, two-phase creatures, doomed to breathe to the rhythm of a beating heart that is older than their breath.

In truth, tracks or traces are forever enigmas, since they appear only in the absence of the beings who have left them behind. Only the presence of those beings would disclose their meaning. It is the traces that are nostalgic, not the anxious beasts who examine them and seek in the depths of their souls the faces that might correspond to them, the names or songs that might call them forth.

De-solidarization and de-synchronization are the condition of those who read and write. Their wit is *Treppenwitz*, 'the wit of the staircase', which leads down to hell.

CHAPTER 49

A Renaissance painter adopted the pseudonym 'Il Morto'. His real name was Pietro Luzzo. Vasari wrote that Morto was an 'original . . . in his brain'; when he had a free moment, he would go down into the vaults of the old city; he would go beneath the ground into the ruins and grottoes of the countryside around Rome to study the remains of Antiquity; this is why he had nicknamed himself 'The Dead One'.

CHAPTER 50

Why a birth without rebirth for humans, whereas plants go on from season to season? Why does the urge suddenly come to a halt in us? Why do we not grow again, as our childhood teeth do? *Pellere, pulsio, poussée*—everything jams up at the age of seven; jams up again at fourteen; we get no taller after twenty-one; everything goes into decline at forty-nine.

*

What drives us to act is a force as distant from consciousness as silence, emotion, sensation and suffering can be.

In *natura*, birth—*nativitas*—stands at the heart of the definition. Anything can be born, as nature's thrust takes it.

The two phases that hunting had merely differentiated, agriculture ranged against each other. We bury and we harvest. Death interred, and life beyond death the following spring.

Agricultural time invented the beyond in the form of the following season. The force that palaeolithic humans admired in wild animals was transformed, in the Neolithic, into the *ch'i* (*qi*) of the Chinese, the *vis* of the Romans, the *phusis* of the Greeks. Floods, storms, lightning were also living beasts. Even the stones were alive. The mountains, too, were animals. There is an imperishable *virtus* of stones, drawing out the greatest of force and feeding it into the longest temporality. This timescale that was 'as long as the life of stones' applied to the veterocracies. The first stone cities were not designed for living people. These entirely dark cities were built for the shades of the dead, the shadow cast by the stars, their light, the hours.

*

Strength: this was the first meaning of virtue. In the *Tusculan Disputations* (II, 22), Cicero wrote: '*Virtus* is the activity of being a *vir* [man], just as *senectus* [old age] is the activity of being a *senex* [old man].' The genitals are called *vires* or, alternatively, *virilia*. *Eviro* means emasculate. *Virtus* is the enactment of the sexual potency proper to the male when he finds himself face to face with the female. Subsequently, it refers to the face-to-face courage of the hero before the threat of the horned beast, signifying the possibility of death. This is what the letter alpha depicts in our tradition: face-to-face (coition), head-to-head (fighting the wild beast), bodily combat, Roman wrestling, Frankish single combat, the mediaeval tournament, the seventeenth-century duel etc. *Vis* is an activity that mingles strength and contempt for death (*fortitudo*) actively, violently. °The *virtus* of a *fascinus*, the virtues (properties) of a plant, the value of a coinage, the meaning of a word—all is *vis*.

*

PASCAL QUIGNARD

Palaeolithically, there is always a force at the heart of every action.

'I was driven by some stronger force.'

This is what heroes say. This is how the subject (the one who says 'I') defines the symptom (the 'I' that is more 'I' than oneself). Some stronger force compelled him. The predatory power of the murderer is like this. So is the demonic violence of the rapist. So is the demiurgic force of the creator. So, in the strict sense, is the *vis* of virtue.

The defiance in the bull and also the sap in the flower are stronger than *they* are. They are *virulent*. *Virus* referred to the sap of plants, to the sperm of mammals or the venom spat by snakes.

*

Paul's genius consisted in inventing resurrection for the whole of humanity. He conceived of a second birth of the body and the spirit after the Last Judgement had been pronounced by God. Before Paul, even Jesus had died. It had taken three days of travails to achieve 'the rebirth of Jesus'. He had to roll the stone away. He had to be recognized by Mary Magdalene. His body had been touched by Thomas' hands. He had to walk to the village of Emmaus, etc.

For Paul, resurrection does not have to do with eternity.

It has to do with the Last Day.

'*In resurrectione*' translates as '*in novissimo die*'.

To re-emerge on the latest day.

Force is stored up; it goes to the newer day; it goes to the newer and newer day.

*

For Paul in Greek, for Augustine in Latin, there is the same haste, the same 'virtue', the same *vis*, the same vernal *stylistic* spirits.

Bounding energy, force, breakthrough, ceaseless impatience, non-generic explosiveness, speculative abruptness.

Vita viva.

*

If Paul invented resurrection, Augustine transformed hell.

Augustine's genius consisted in transporting the subterranean wandering of poor shades in black togas, gradually sinking into a swamp of stagnant water, into a sedentary, urban life in a celestial imperial city of sempiternal light. He transformed the abyss of impotent, exhausted, enfeebled human life into a sparkling, virulent, eternal future. He transformed the mortal destiny of a groaning ghost into the promised immortalization of a *corpus gloriosum*. In this way, a divine city became the 'meaning' of every earthly town. Urban communities grew up around the tombs of the saints protecting cemeteries. In the case of Saint Martin, the city was Tours. With Saint Cassius, it was Bonn, etc.

CHAPTER 51

The Boat with the Black Flames

In Normandy, in my childhood, a simple chair covered with a white cloth, which was set down at a crossroads, was called a *paradis de port de mer*. Pinned against the back of it, a pious engraving was surrounded by little vases containing flowers. Candles were lit and placed in front of the engraving. Wax dripped from them and stuck to the straw of which the chair seat was made.

The engraving depicted a boat in a storm.

God standing on the waves had his hands raised over the sea.

The boat in the *paradis de port de mer* is the boat of the dead, *circumdata ignibus atris*. It is the boat on the Styx, 'surrounded by black flames'.

Only these 'black' flames, invisible in the night of the living since they merge with the stellar obscurity, can cast a light in the darkness of hell.

All his life, Paul Celan scribbled drawings of candles, burnt down to varying degrees, in the margins of his poems.

In days gone by, twenty millennia ago, positive handprints looked like nothing so much as flames at the end of torches.

The male organ, when it desires, when it rises on the masculine body, resembles a flame spurting out at the end of a strange branch.

A flame in the form of the male organ appeared to Ocrisia and Queen Tanaquil: °then Servius Tullius was born.

°In a painting by Georges de La Tour, exhibited in the Palais du Louvre, the fingers of the infant Jesus, surrounding a flame in the night, seem like a flower.

CHAPTER 52

On the Power Inherent in the Colour Black

Rata had a strange dream, since it was one in which he saw nothing. He saw nothing at all. He was lost in the most opaque darkness. It was night within night. This terrible darkness woke him. Then Rata spoke to himself, saying: 'Oh, my eyes are closed! How black everything is! My dream is one of demolition.' Then he got up from his bed and Rata said farewell to his country with these words: 'Oh my country, hide your face because you no longer have a face for me! Be lost, lost! Lost now during my farewell! Lost later during my journey!' Once he had spoken these words, Rata dragged his boat down to the water; put out to sea; paddled and paddled. He did not turn round and, indeed, no longer saw his country. Everything was black. Once Rata had left he never returned.

CHAPTER 53

Pompey

He donned a dark toga and hid his face. He slipped into the shadows. He ran off without a word. Behind him six thousand of his soldiers lay dead on the battlefield. He was thirty-four years old. He skirted the city of Larissa. He came to the river known as the Tempè. He got down on his knees to drink. He saw fishermen. He purchased their boat from them. He followed the river down to the sea where he found a cargo ship just about to weigh anchor. He boarded it immediately. He reached Amphipolis and from there took another vessel to get to Mytilene, in order to pick up Cornelia and his son who were waiting for him. He dispatched a longboat with a letter for his wife informing her that if she wanted to see Pompey defeated, vanquished, poor and wholly alone on a single ship that did not even belong to him, she should get into the longboat. She should come to him. Cornelia and her son accepted and came. Pompey hugged his wife and, weeping, told her: 'Wife, a demon has drawn us on to a road that is different from the one that was. We have passed out of former times and into the present.' The sailors hoisted the sails. The ship reached Attalia where it was joined by Cilician triremes. They came within sight of the Egyptian coast. Pompey dropped anchor. He asked Ptolemy for help. Ptolemy immediately called a meeting of his council. Pothinus the Eunuch said: 'We should drive him away.' Achillas the Officer said: 'We should welcome him.' Theodotos the Rhetor said: 'If we welcome him, Caesar will become our enemy and Pompey will be our master. If we drive him away, Pompey will accuse us of having rejected him and Caesar of having let him depart. We must have him come to us and kill him.' Ptolemy hesitated. Theodotos the Rhetor then added: 'A corpse does not bite.' Ptolemy then ratified Theodotos' decision and entrusted its execution to Achillas.

Achillas came out in a boat to Pompey's ship and called out: 'It's too silted up for a trireme to come and fetch you. Get into this boat.'

Pompey hesitated. He eventually got into the boat with the aid of ropes. Once aboard he turned back to the ship. He shouted to Cornelia: 'We have passed from time past to time present.'

He grasped the hand that Philippus held out to him to help him sit, and Septimius, behind him, took advantage of this to run him through with his sword. His head was cut off by Achillas. Theodotos the Rhetor kept Pompey's severed head. His naked body was thrown from the boat into the sea. Two days later an old Roman walking on the beach, fishing for octopus, took pity on the headless body the waves brought in. He wrapped it in a tunic. He burnt it in the remains of a fishing boat that had washed up on the shore.

CHAPTER 54

Arriving in darkness at the gates of the underworld, Aeneas first encountered the *insepulti*. *Insepulti* was the name the Romans gave to those who had not been buried in the earth by the survivors. They were doomed to wander for a hundred years on the banks of the Styx, where they roamed as vagabonds or bandits before they were able to rob a recently deceased man and steal a gold coin to pay for their passage through oblivion.

Then Aeneas encountered the souls of dead children. These were called the *aörai*.

Aeneas then suddenly came face to face with the shades that had suffered violent deaths. These last pre-infernal shades were subdivided into four classes: the men condemned to death; those who had committed suicide out of despair or extreme suffering; the lovers who had killed themselves for love or committed murder while in the grip of passion; the warriors who had died in combat but whose bones had not been gathered up (*legein, relegere, eligere*) on the battlefield or, in the course of a naval battle, from the sea.

All were banned from the underworld.

For the ancient world, the *insepulti* were literally *u-topias*: bodies without a place. Dead children were *ana-chronisms*: in them, time had got out of joint. For the victims of violent death, it wasn't the violence that was being punished in their exclusion from the Underworld but their disappearance before their time. The absurd concept of the 'prematurely dead' is needed to define the group of these half-angels, half-demons left hanging round on the fringes of the Underworld. These souls wander about until the number of years for which their lives *should have* run is reached.

Sometimes, insufficient farewells are made.

Even if all the dyings of men are unfinishable, there are some dead men who are more unfinished than others.

Hence the 'unfinished life' wanders the world of the living like an unused force waiting for someone to grasp it and complete it.

The psychical time of still fevered souls hangs in the air.

Dead men who are not yet completely dead wander all around. This isn't a story. It is everyday life. They are seen in every dream. They are repeated in every decision.

*

So many unpredictable demonries, whose unfocussed vitality, curtailed germination, suppressed aggression, unslaked thirst, unquenched appetite, unsated desire and unrealized fecundity can be used against the living.

Medea avenged herself with premature deaths (of her two sons whom she ran through with a sword), so that the resultant avenging spirits would rage against Jason and persecute him endlessly. Admittedly, the kinship and youth of the victims are cruel elements in Medea's crime but, beside the family ties and even beside their youth, it was the still seething vitality that was of importance to her, enabling her to unleash an intense, 'viral', lastingly virulent vengeance on her husband. By cutting her children's throats, Medea was manufacturing demons.

In Rome, virgins were raped before they were killed so that their frustrated fecundity would be less harmful over time.

*

Even after becoming a Christian in Tunisia, Tertullian wrote: 'Souls that have not known sexual delight are filled with the spite produced by the life they have not known. Their leftover fecundity turns them bad.' This is what the German philosophers called *Sehnsucht*, dangerous nostalgia. It is fearful sentimentality.

*

To be able to relate what he lived through (to express what he had to live through on the extraordinary porous frontier of death) in the Kolyma camps, Varlam Shalamov split himself into two characters, one of whom dies, while the other lives on.

Shalamov was able to say what he had been made to suffer only by depicting characters that were 'living dead'.

Trying to fit parts that were irrevocably dead into parts that survived.

*

At the beginning of the *Eudemian Ethics*, Aristotle defines courage as a spasm grafted onto duration. The impulse that is at the origin of the initial willed action opts for time. Courage is not a moment that lasts: it is its very upsurge that has to be reproduced continuously.

This is a strange graft which is, in truth, impossible for humans.

Courage desires 'irruption without intermittence'.

If the 'heart' is blood pulsing rhythmically, 'having heart' supposes an energy that is more stable in its beginnings, more continuous in its inflow.

Courage in human beings is perhaps the opposite of desire.

If courage could exist in the pure state in human beings, it would be an even wildness, without jumps or jolts—a domesticated wildness—entirely willed, sustained, slow. It is the opposite of the brief, unpredictable, rapidly exhausted wildness of sexual joltings. Courage and desire are both relentless. In a man who desires there is something that cannot be finished off. In a corpse there is something that is not finished off. This is why we have to include in the definition of courage the virtue of finishing off. This power of accomplishment adds the 'mortal blow' to death. It is art. To know how to finish off is the secret of art.

*

To know how to finish off is to derive, out of putting-to-death itself, something to kill what, in death, remains of life. Only those with 'courage' can make this sacrifice. Knowing how to finish a work, knowing how to break off a love affair requires courage and an emphatic rapidity that is not loquacious but abrupt. A deliberate abruptness. I am touching here on the mystery of the craftsman's courage. Dürer is the one who knows how to withdraw his hand before making one stroke too many. For an ancient Greek thinker, courage is something that continues to surge, that draws on the surging movement in the depths of nature (in the depths of volcanoes, tides, winds, lightning, earthquakes). °*Phusis* has its forerunner in *rhusis*. Being has its forerunner in Time. The courageous man is that strange artisan of time and death who *applies himself* to that movement which outruns time itself. Protagoras set above piety and even above wisdom the courage of beginnings, tenacity in practice and the time that knows how to interrupt eagerness without deflecting from its course the drive that carries it forward. Courage is an incaution that fears as greatly as caution may do but *nonetheless* puts its nose outside, leaves its cover, suddenly spins around and faces up to things. It drives on, come what may. As a consequence of this valiant incautiousness, courage is silence. It goes back to the halting or suspension of movement that guides the action of wild animals, when suddenly they prick up their ears and a troubled look comes over them. That halting is a pulling back to leap. It is a *mimesis* that goes back to long before natural languages. It is not a human organic virtue. It is a reflective onrushing which, at the moment of decision, at the moment of the temporal *initium*, has to be unreflective. The Japanese samurai and poets in their extraordinary middle ages meditated as no one else in the world has done on this 'bold moment'—this suspended time that suddenly unleashes itself. It is a question of taking back from nature and animality their unconscious springings-forth. Becoming abrupt. Pouncing. Uttering a little cry. Becoming searing as lightning. Putting the final touch. Striking the chord.

CHAPTER 55

°Franz Süssmayr: 'I complete the masterpieces which death interrupted or which their authors left unfinished at the point where their strength had deserted them.'

CHAPTER 56

'Not even in dreams can one possess the time that dispossesses,' writes Philodemus of Herculaneum. The Neapolitan philosopher goes on more strangely: 'One should not wish men long life, for long life is not lively life.'

What the men of antiquity and the slopes of Vesuvius called lively life is not what Rimbaud and the rainy forests of the Ardennes called 'true life'. Where this Greek sentence penned by Philodemus is concerned, we should also remember that it was the force of a volcano and the power of its lava that preserved it from the slow ravages of time and the religious, hate-filled violence of men.

Life is an intensity, time is a measure.

It matters little that a life be long or short, all that counts are the maximal moments (the spurtings of the Erstwhile) in full presence (on the shores of the earth).

Just as all that counts in each person's body is the empty, free, alert, lightly bounding *intimum*, not the ego or the image or the power of words taught by others.

The Erstwhile is the increscible—and the course of time that unfolds it is disordered and uncertain.

In former times, the Epicureans of Pompeii, Herculaneum, Paestum and Capri invoked this argument so as not to put off any joy until the morrow.

'*Carpe diem*,' wrote Horace most audaciously when Augustus imposed his tyrannical power and invented the empire. Horace lived in a little alleyway in Rome that was never again to be as overpopulated as it was then. The point is to grab a little sickle, so as to pluck a day from time, as though one were plucking a flower from nature. Sever the day! Geld the hour! Decide to cut down this *Tuesday*, for example, as though it were a *peony*. With each dawn, the Erstwhile propels a new light into space. No two dawns are the same. All the world's mornings never recur. No two nights are alike. Each night is the depth of space incarnate. No two flowers, two dews, two lives are alike. We must at every moment say: thou. To all that comes we must say: let it come. Life is a single moment of *re-citatio* that springs forth at each of its points, that refines its happiness with each life-renewing occasion. A joy increasingly clear of troubles and fears, though not entirely of primal distress. Presence, days, flowers, points, bodies, cries, joy can all be concentrated down.

CHAPTER 57

Experiri

The humans afflicted with Alois Alzheimer's disease taught me of the muddled, empty Greater Time that meanders beneath time. Their troubled—almost immortal—wisdom is total. They are almost children. This wisdom without consciousness or reference points is totally disabling. Disorientation has overtaken it.

Time is not a transcendental datum. Time is not a mental form that precedes experience. The temporal relation is a socially constructed interhuman relation, whose origin is agricultural, whose functions are religious and which is as acquired as language is, and can be lost just as language can be destroyed on men's lips. But the onrushing totality of the upthrust is not lost when that relation is destroyed. Human time can without doubt be analysed as a construction of interlocking timescales that are tricky to learn, easy to erode and quick to be obliterated: the identification of successions, the build-up of changes, the collection of time spans, limits, memories, forgetting, faces, deaths. I want, *however*, to study this *little remainder*: the blossoming of a lasting relationship in the representation humans make for themselves of what is lost. The void before birth. The black hole before the sun. Here the irruption of the unforeseeable, which is a feature of being lost in the human world of objects, unfolds its own specific time. It is this time of mourning, so lasting and durable as it is, so unfinishable and aoristic, that creates the space for art. °Franz Kafka wrote to Oskar Pollak in 1904: 'We need books that affect us like the death of someone we loved more than ourselves.'

*

We need narratives because each person being born was once a completely lost hero.

*

The construction of a 'more internal' linguistic 'pocket' in the human brain unfurls from the site of the speech function.

It is this empty site that death comes to inhabit.

The daily exercise of *meditatio mortis* among the Romans of the empire shows the degree to which, for them, the end could never be situated in one's last moments.

*

We are fated to our first life, which is forgotten with the advent of respiration. In the dazzle of the light of birth the initial darkness fades. A first life omitted from language, to the point where we don't even date our lives from the beginning of our lives.

We claim to date from our birth.

Being born and immediately forced into retrospectiveness.

Then into the time that is acquired with the acquisition of language.

The Latin verb *ex-periri* means *sur*-vive. French *faire l'expérience de* really means 'to attempt to re-experience'.

Schritt zurück, breakdown, *regressus ad uterum*, *regressio mentis*—all these debts, all these retrocessions are imposed (1) by foetal life before atmospheric life, (2) by the *infantia* that precedes acquired natural language.

*

Duchamp called his pictures '*les retards*'—delays. The time lag was one generation for the elite, two generations for the educated spectator and three generations for the general public. It took a century before crowds gathered in entire unanimity to admire the national hero (the religious martyr) invented by historical narration in a process of retrospective judgement.

*

Kinship is linguistic in the sense that it is exclusively retroactive. Every genealogy is the product of a narrative that founds rather than explains it. The name one bears tells a story that older human beings reported even as they contrived it. It is a legend that is placed upon a little non-speaking, living animal.

Those of the previous generation give each child that is born a dead person's name and baptize it as part of an old, mendacious—or, at least, greatly enhanced—history.

Not to name is to not cause to be born; it is to break the chain; it is to prevent access to the status of ancestor in the passing-on of the name, just as it is to prevent access to the revenant in the baptism in which his name was intending to return.

*

The body of the foetus experiences as something lost the interior body in which it lived before it distinguished itself therefrom, before it escaped, before, in the moments following birth, it suddenly discovered that body as standing over against its own—in front

203

of its eyes, to its utmost surprise and dismay—as the body of its mother. The infant is like a little lost object beside a big object it has left. This is how fusion becomes hostility. When the mourner gives the deceased a precious object to take with him into the earth, it is a token. Something other than the lost one must depart with the loss. And what remains must not fuse again with the lost one. These two pitfalls are two deaths which the sacrifice avoids. It is possible that the sacrifice of the mourning, which precedes *Sapiens Sapiens*, forms the basis for the specifically human sacrifice in the share-outs that follow hunting, since a dead creature is again involved: in this case, the prey that is killed and cut up. Animals provide the foundation for sacrifice in an active sharing of the spoils and an extraordinarily deferential temporal division. First comes the carnivore. Then the winged carrion feeder. After the winged carrion feeders come the terrestrial ones: jackals, hyenas, wolves and dogs. And lastly human beings.

CHAPTER 58

What did Saint Peter forsake? One's inclination is to say that Saint Peter forsook only the boat and the net. But Peter said to the Lord:

ᵒBehold, Lord, we have forsaken all.

'Reliquimus *omnia*.'

It was not merely the boat and the net Saint Peter forsook: he forsook everything. In forsaking the boat and the net, he forsook transport and predation. In other words, he forsook transference and the bond. In abandoning transport, transference, predation and bonds, everything was forsaken.

The chrysanthemum was brought to Toulouse by Captain Bernet in 1831.

The invasion of all of France's cemeteries by pots of chrysanthemums on All Souls' Day was completed in 1880.

It is easy to remember the date. °It was the day the Lion of Belfort was erected.

Every human being, as he is born, loses the envelope that contained him. The bond is broken as soon as the umbilical cord is cut. Then what has been cut is knotted. In this way, live fusion has been, successively, *cut* and *formed*.

The placenta is thrown in the bin. The remains of the cord are thrown in the bin. The bond is lost.

It is not only the mother who is a lost breast and a lost womb.

A possibility of engulfment roams around in matter.

'Strangelets' is the name given to the newborn aggregates that are capable of swallowing up older atomic nuclei.

In this way, certain planets are digested by more unstable varieties of the matter that is so plentiful in space.

CHAPTER 61

It so happened that when the emperor Alexander arrived in heaven an incredibly heavy skull was placed in his hands. His arms immediately drooped, his back buckled and, so heavy was the skull, he had to lay it down on the ground. So the emperor of the Greeks could not enter paradise and remained on the threshold.

He meditated for two days.

On the third day he bent down and picked up a little earth in his fingers. He mingled his spittle with that earth. He carefully stopped up the two empty eye sockets in the cranium. Then he picked up the skull as though it were a feather and put it under his arm. He murmured:

'In truth, the skulls of dead men are no heavier than a handful of dry earth.'

And he made to enter paradise.

But a tombless warrior who was waiting there held him back, asking him how it was that the skulls of the dead could suddenly become so light when you stopped up their eye sockets with dust mingled with spittle.

Alexander the Conqueror replied to the *insepultus*:

'In man, the only thing of weight is his insatiable eye.'

CHAPTER 62

They slipped a sachet containing herbs under the pillows of the dead so that their bodies would be protected right up to their resurrection on the Day of Wrath. These sachets were lists of qualia. The lists turned into little verses. I can reel off the Wirzwisch list from memory: 'Hart's-tongue, nightshade, artemisia, St John's-wort, parsley, centaury, herb-bennet, rue, sage, savory, time.'

It's a very fine poem for speaking out loud rather than for reading, its initial movement slow, its latter movement rapid.

And for sensing rather than speaking.

*

Time was suspended. The clocks were stopped, large and small, together with watches and alarm clocks. They were only wound up again when people came back from the cemetery.

*

So long as the corpse was in the house, something of a life still floated in the air. People spoke softly. They held their breath and toned down their gestures. The whole family was part of this being-between-two-worlds. They gave the soul as much help as they could while it was still hesitating between time and eternity. Once the breath had gone out of it, the soul had to ascend into the blue sky. It mustn't be tempted to stay near to the heart and the sadness and the regret and the memory and the bed and the hearth and the barrel and the chest. Nothing should hold back those who must depart. They closed the blinds. They pulled down the shutters. They covered the mirrors, looking glasses and shiny objects. The plates on the narrow shelves of the dresser were turned to the wall. All the copper pans were turned around. The fire was put out. The water in the well was covered up, as was the milk.

A strip of the shroud was worn on clothing (a mourning band) and put on musical instruments and doors. They put a cover over the fishtank on top of the closed piano.

Birdcages were covered up.

In the area around Metz, on the death of the head of the family, the heir went down into the cellar to tell the wine the master was dead. The surviving son went from barrel to barrel. He tapped three times with his finger, telling each barrel: '*Uwen meester is dood*.'

At the other end of France, the same thing was done with the beehives: three taps of the finger in the sunshine.

The beekeeper walked to the other end of the field and mumbled into the air around his face: '*Revelhatz-vous, petitas, lou mestre est mort*.' Wake up little ones, the master is dead.

CHAPTER 63

Aemilianus the Rhetor had Epitherses for his father. One day, in the reign of Tiberius, as Epitherses was on his way to Italy, the Egyptian vessel on which he was travelling found itself suddenly becalmed in the seas around the Echinades.

It was still daylight.

On the boat the passengers were eating; they were playing dice; they were whispering to one another when they suddenly heard a distant voice coming from the islands of Paxos.

The voice said clearly: 'Thamus, Thamus!'

The passengers fell silent.

Thamus was the name of the Egyptian pilot manning the helm. At the third calling of his name, Thamus could no longer control himself. He let go of the helm and threw himself face down on the deck to honour the god addressing him before all the passengers and pronouncing his name so distinctly. Then the mysterious voice was heard again, saying, 'Thamus, when you come opposite to Palodes, announce that the god Pan is dead.'

Thamus remained prostrate on the deck but the voice spoke no more. The wind picked up again. The ship moved on into the night that had fallen as the voice was speaking. Then Thamus got back to his feet and took the helm once more. When the vessel had reached Palodes, the wind fell again. On this occasion Thamus took his time. He dropped anchor, came slowly to the stern and standing with his face turned towards the land, he cried out in Greek: '*O megas Pan tethnèken.*' Great Pan is dead.

At that moment was heard, rising from the earth, a great sob uttered by thousands, mingled with cries of surprise.

*

Plutarch means to say that when the gods speak no longer, something more ancient and less grandiloquent wells up.

This is what he calls a great sob.

Megas stenagmos. A great groan.

Men are groaning, filled with surprise at how intense their own pain can be.

As they fade from the scene, the gods give way to that which gave rise to them. The gods are originally sobs rising to the lips. They are pure appeals.

The Sirens too were pure appeals upon the sea.

CHAPTER 64

A Greek epigraph was dug up at Rome in 1878.

There is in Hades neither boat, nor boatman Charon, nor guardian Aeacus.

In the Underworld there are only

Bones, names, ashes.

CHAPTER 65

De atheismo

To live without god is an extreme human possibility. It is not actually the impious individual who is condemned in the atheist but the traitor to the group. This is why the chronicle of atheism is a history of continuous, endless persecution. Theodorus Atheus was banished by the Areopagus. Yang Chu was killed. Wang Chaung was persecuted. Later, the Greek *atheos* was translated into Latin as *sine deo*. As regards what drives the spirit, I think atheism is impossible, since it is not possible wholly to wrest a humanity which speaks from the verbal hallucination and abstract ideas that gradually emanate from words. More than this, it is impossible to wrench mammals from nocturnal dreaming without driving them mad. No animal's body can escape the two great hallucinations of hunger and desire.

Unbelief can only be an effort, and also an act of courage.

ºGabriel Le Bras said: 'The sociology of irreligion is the most moving chapter in the history of groups.'

It is certainly the most heroic.

It is also the shortest.

*

I term 'atheist' the person who lives without gods, whose soul is without faith, whose consciousness is exempt from fear, whose morals are not based on rites, whose thought is exempt from any reference to god, devil, demon, hallucination, love or obsession, whose death is accessible to the idea of suicide, whose post-death is nothingness.

In a sermon he preached in 1551 in Paris beside the fortress of the Louvre at the church of Saint-Germain l'Auxerrois, François le Picard declared: 'The people called *athei* are *sine deo*. They live oblivious of God.'

In 1551 Geoffroy Vallée was born in Orleans. He wrote *De arte nihil credendi*. He had it printed at his own expense and published it in his own name. Both Vallée and his book were burnt on 9 February 1574.

*

°*De arte nihil credendi* was written in late adolescence, as was La Boétie's *Contr'un*. He is full of that counter-nostalgia, that *Sehnsucht*, that vague, effervescent aspiration, that elan that is so uncertain because he is not yet aware that his search is genital.

De arte nihil credendi: On the art of 'believing' in nothingness. A more exact translation would be: On the capacity to believe in nothing.

Vallée's discovery: nihilism is a treasure.

God is a pure nothing (*purum nihil*).

A mere name (*mera vox*).

A purely vocal sound floating in the air like the cry of a bird (*flatus vocis*).

An abstract idea (*fictum quid*).

Vallée, La Boétie, Rimbaud—extraordinary, peremptory geniuses. Vallée is twenty-four when he dies at the stake.

Vallée is the first libertine.

°It was Gentillet who, in the late sixteenth century, stated that being an atheist was synonymous with being 'literary'.

Atheists are men of letters.

More precisely, Gentillet wrote in 1576: 'Atheistic people are betrayed by their libraries.'

Gentillet gives the list of the books that library includes: 'Those who possess in their homes the books of the following are atheistic men: Democritus, Epicurus, Lucretius, Pliny, Lucian, Martial, Tibullus, Catullus, Propertius, Ovid, Porphyry, Alexander, Averroes, Poggio, Boccaccio, Guido Aretinus, Petrarch, Machiavelli, Pomponazzi, Cardano.'

*

If atheism is the most difficult stage it has been given to human mental experience to know, then that value (or at least that doubting of all values) is all the more inestimable for the fact that victory always lies beyond its grasp.

Doubting was born with writing.

The spacing which doubt presupposes is a product of the dislocation of the linguistic flow in written letters.

The dislocation of the linguistic flow in written letters enables the following to be decontextualized: seasons, ages, kings, myths, gods, chronicles, heroes, experiences, genres.

*

Stevenson signed his letters, 'The Atheist'.

*

We may add endlessly to the list Gentillet had begun to draw up: Meslier, Sade, Stendhal, Mérimée, Baudelaire, Thomas Hardy, Marx, Engels,

Schopenhauer, Nietzsche, Freud, Mallarmé, Valéry, Bataille, Lacan.

*

To be an atheist is: (1) to become heretical once again in respect of every religion; (2) to be an apostate from all religions.

It is to be a living and breathing schism.

In the sixteenth century, in the seventeenth century, in the eighteenth century, in the nineteenth century, in the twentieth century, in the twenty-first century, literary people recognized their own kind. °They leant over and murmured: '*De tribus impostoribus*!' Moses, Jesus, Mohammed seemed to them to be tyrannical masters laying claim to the totality of the social field. The dogmas the three prophets had advanced had contrived a control over people's souls, which they hemmed in with prescriptions and terrors. They taxed resources to keep leaders in the lap of luxury who, century after century, took millions and tens of millions of bodies and sacrificed them in crusades or martyrdom.

*

Five letters in capitals: FICTA

°Pirithous the Atheist said: '*Ficta*. They are fables. The gods are without power.'

*

Euhemerus the Atheos had written: 'Zeus is an old king who came and died on Crete.'

*

Seven little letters in lower case: *écr l'inf*. These seven mysterious *litterae 'écr l'inf'* emanating from Voltaire's pen and placed at the end of certain of his letters meant: *Il faut écraser l'infâme*—we must crush the Beast; we must set aside superstition, we must destroy faith, we must root out fanaticism.

He grew old.

On 9 January 1777, a now senile Voltaire went back to Paris after twenty-eight years of absence to meet Benjamin Franklin. ⁰He turned to the eldest of Benjamin Franklin's grandchildren who was called Temple. He placed his hands on his head. He blessed him, saying in English: 'God and Liberty.'

The democracy of the United States of America retained God in its oaths, institutions, teaching, festivals and money. The banknotes still bear the legend 'In God We Trust.' The oath of allegiance still contains the phrase 'One Nation under God.' At the beginning of the twenty-first century, American citizens still referred to the area that voted twice for the name of Bush as the 'Bible Belt'.

I want first to recall the wonderful complaint of the gods in Lucian: 'We, the gods, tremble. We always tremble. We tremble, as bulls, for fear of being sacrificed. We tremble, when golden, for fear of being melted down . . .'

*

The first '*Gott ist tot*' scene is in the last pages of *Siebenkäs*. Jean Paul's novel was published in 1796.

Jesus, in a cemetery, is urged by the corpses of men surrounding him to tell them:

'Is God still alive?'

Jesus does not know how to go about telling the corpses the news he bears.

'Christ, is there no God?'

°Jesus said to them: 'There is none.'

But the shades of the dead were not satisfied with this answer. They continued to harass him. Eventually Jesus said:

'I have looked everywhere, on earth, in the seas, throughout the universe. °We are orphans. You, I, we are orphans. There is no father.'

°The second 'God is dead' scene is found in Quinet in 1833. 'Ahasuerus, good Ahasuerus, tell us the name we are looking for! And when I replied, "Is it Christ?" they repeated the name with a snigger. "Christ? No, he is too old for us. The earth no longer throws up new gods to meet our hunger".'

The third '*Gott ist tot*' scene is from Heinrich Heine. It was published in the *Revue des Deux Mondes* on 15 November 1834. 'Do you not hear the little bell tinkling? On your knees! They are administering the sacraments to a dying god.' Heine names Kant, in Germany, as 'God's murderer'. He adds: 'This gloomy piece of news will perhaps take a few centuries to spread to all parts.'

The fourth '*Gott ist tot*' scene is Max Stirner's. This scene is the closest to the one conceived by Geoffroy Vallée in 1572. Max Stirner wrote in 1844: 'We have killed God, but Man exists no more than God exists. There remains the Unique one, which rests on the Ephemeral, a mortal creation that devours itself and I say, ° "*Ich hab' mein Sac' auf Nichts gestellt.*"' 'I have taken nothingness as my cause.'

Quinet's *Ahasvérus* predates Nietzsche's *Zarathustra* by fifty years. We have to read the sentence Nietzsche wrote in 1883 to its very end: '*Gott ist tot! Und wir haben ihn getötet! Ist nicht die Grösse dieser Tat zu gross für uns?*' 'God is dead! We killed him! Is not the grandeur of that act too great for us?'

This fifth scene is the decisive one. We have to break down this sacrifice into three sequences, assembled positively in Nietzsche's thought.

God is dead. This is the culmination of the Christian world. The Christian world can be summed up as follows: God became a dying man by two methods: he was first made flesh and, after having been tortured and nailed to a slave's cross, died.

We killed him. It wasn't just the Romans who crucified him. It wasn't just the Jews who called for his death, the Christians adored his death, the Christians painted his death, the Christians sculpted his death, the Christians hymned his death throughout the entire history of their religion. Take Luther's cruel commentary: 'God as God died in the sacrifice of Jesus.' °Hegel wrote in the *Phenomenology of Spirit* of Luther's 'hard saying that "God is dead"'.

Is not the grandeur of that act too great for us? Yes. We have to believe that the grandeur of that act is too great for us, since so many men in the last four centuries have been terrified by nihilism.

For example, all philosophers are horrified by nihilism.

For example, the successive exterminations of the megafauna, then of the gods, then of nature, then of the human essence of men are never conceived as part of a single process.

CHAPTER 68

The Four Theses

The four theses.

First thesis. The return of the pious calls for the return of atheists. (Only when unbelief was on the increase could atheism be regarded as useless.)

Second thesis. The reappearance of bloody wars of religion demands that they be contested irreligiously.

Third thesis. The irrationalism of the late twentieth century calls for a new detoxification. (It was Marx who in January 1844 wrote these two sentences that are themselves so strange in their formulation, inasmuch as he juxtaposes them: 'Religion is the sigh of the oppressed creature . . . It is the opium of the people.')

Fourth thesis. As sexual puritanism makes a comeback, so libertines must make a comeback. (Only what is sexual is the real revenant. It is to sleep that we owe an awakening. The sexual is the only 'living' source of all bodies. And it is the sexual erection that reawakens the body as dreaming ends.)

°When she appeared before the Fourth War Council, Louise Michel explained radically: 'Liberated, libertines, libertarians, free people—gentlemen, make no distinction. We are atheists, for we wish to be free.'

*

The four definitions.

Neutrality might be said to consist in not taking sides in a war, *but atheism is a war.*

Tolerance might be said to consist in not taking sides between religions, *but by mysteriously equating all faiths, simple unbelief validates them all.*

In atheism *lucidity* is wrested without any possible hope, any possible peace, from credulity. (This is an endless, incomplete, interminable, impossible, infinite liberation.)

Loss of illusion is to be preferred to *belief* and *truth*.

*

Lucidity may be regarded as a higher value than illusion. But however this may be, and however little we may like it, the desire to believe is reborn like sleep or thirst, or like the attachment of love or the desire to be happy.

He who is lost calls on the ersatz, hunger calls on dreams, the brain calls on language and the speaker calls on lies, *as the child calls on the mother*.

CHAPTER 69

Superstitiosi, Religiosi, People in Mourning

The Roman definition of *superstitio* is found in Cicero: °Those men are termed superstitious (*super-stitiosi*) who immolate victims so that their children may survive them (*superstites*). Hence Cicero contrasts *superstitiosi* with *religiosi*. Those persons are termed *religiosi* who gather together (*relegere*) the things that appertain to the worship of the gods. Freud speaks of those whom Cicero calls *superstitiosi* as *Trauernde—people in mourning*. Death takes with it the gaze of the loved one, leaving the survivor suddenly bereft of that gaze. For those deprived of it, the absence of the gaze that was directed at them is like a night. The shade of the dead person mingles with that night, crushes the ego, wastes it, gnaws away at it. In this way, the one walking in darkness falls prey to the missing gaze as he is increasingly, harrowingly and obscurely swallowed up by it. The lost one thus devours the *superstes* (the survivor), dragging him down with him into the realm of the *umbrae* (the shades). °Saint-Evremond said the world of the living was merely another hell situated between earth and moon.

Theorem. The forsakenness of the living is never greater than the distress of the shades.

*

The an-aetiological and a-teleological character of atheistic thought unhooks the psyche from social functioning. The sequences in the atheists' novels lacking all cause and purpose distance them from groups. Though cities, divinities, languages, masses and wars are inherent, atheism leads fatally to individualism; the atheist is an outsider; always alone; always defenceless; always victim; always burnt. This question of the fragility of atheists and men of letters was already a problem for Taoism and Buddhism several centuries before the religion of Jesus arose in Palestine and spread into the empire of the Romans, to the point where it shrouded that empire in gloom, progressively swallowed it up as prey, devouring it whole to the point of making it entirely its own.

*

If you step aside from war, you step aside from polities; you step aside from history; you step aside from the gods.

CHAPTER 70

Immortalia ne speres

Not to hope for immortal things—

that is the advice afforded by the hour,

by days, seasons, the year. Spring

repairs the trees after winter. We, human beings,

once we have descended to where the ancient kings
    of Rome lie,

have no one to come looking for us beneath the Earth
    and we do not re-grow.

Not even Tullus or Ancus or Orpheus are waiting for
    us, mingled with the sand of the riverbank.

°That there were somewhere Manes and a kingdom
    to which they went,

That there was a dark world below the grasses and
   fields,

That one saw Charon's pole among the reeds looming
   up out of the darkness,

Saw his white buttocks and the bark,

That this single bark was sufficient to transport so
   many thousands of dead,

That the prow of the bark was ceaselessly coming and
   going from the shore of this world to the far shore
   of the other,

These things not even children believe.

°This is what Juvenal said in *Satires II*, 149.

It was very fine weather in the late afternoon of 29 June 1670. °Henrietta Anne of England, who was at Saint-Cloud, asked for a glass of chilled chicory water and immediately felt she was dying. They informed Bossuet, who was there. Or who was, at least, reading in the gardens, in a canvas chair in the shade. Madame de La Fayette was given the task of undressing Henrietta Anne, so that she could don a ceremonial robe for her last moment. Madame de La Fayette touched, embraced and kissed the arm of her friend, while gently slipping off the material. At that moment, Henrietta passed an Inuit remark to Madame de La Fayette. It was, in fact, the last word she spoke:

'My nose has already gone.'

°Never mind the marvellous words spoken by Bossuet. Henrietta said: 'It seems to me my nose has already gone.' The Inuit touch their noses. They pull on them to prove they are not dead. They pull on them and have them pulled as evidence that they have not become spirits, ghosts, demons. To prove that their noses have not fallen off, as one sees on the faces of the dead when tombs are opened.

CHAPTER 72

Spitting blood, dragged along on my hospital trolley on 27 January 1997, with my body thrown back in response to the haemorrhagic violence that was rising from the depths of my lungs and shooting out from my lips in great spurts, I was beginning to die. I discovered that it was pleasant to die. There is an ecstasy of dying. The ancient Greeks spoke of an *apatheia* of farewell. I passed Jérôme Equer in the basements of the Saint-Antoine hospital and we did not see one another, even though we crossed on the same day at the same time, laid out on our stretchers. The two friends were dying on the same date. They say that bamboos from the same parent plant flower on the same date and die on the same date, however far apart in the world they are planted.

In the Gironde, the unhappy dead indicated the number of masses they needed to get into Paradise by imprinting their bloody hands the requisite number of times on the wall.

They were making an appeal.

The soul appeals not for its repose (in the Other world) but rather for its remaining (in Strength).

In the suttee sacrifice the Indian widow immolates herself on her husband's body, after first leaving the red imprint of her hand on the entrance to the house. This is the *object* she leaves from her sacrifice (the painted trace of her blood, from her body that has disappeared in the flames).

Jocasta kills herself on the threshold of the palace of Thebes. Before falling, she places her bloody hand on Oedipus' house. This is a suttee directed towards Oedipus. Jocasta is thereby affirming that he is, above all, her husband (before being her son). But Oedipus was not a man to be hailed by the wife in the woman. He loved the mother in the woman.

The red *sub sole* begs for the black *in utero*.

*

The first man had a mouth red with blood. The Romans said of him: 'The first man was the first atheist.'

Opening his blood-filled mouth he said to the other men: *Experiar deus hic*. I am going to put a god to the test (I shall eat the god and that god will be full of blood like men). And he opened his mouth and it was, in fact, full of blood. Then the gods wished for the doom of the human race that had stolen their secret. Man became wolf because he had given man to man to eat. This is why the first man, among the Romans, was called Wolf: Lykaon. Face of violence: *Violentiae vultus*. °Image of pride: *Imago feritatis*.

*

Pentheus, beaten to death by his mother, his limbs torn from him, was devoured raw, while still alive, as only mothers can do when they eat their young.

His mother finally ripped off his head. She held it by the hair. She questioned her son's head, as it dripped with blood. She called upon it:

'Go on! Dare to tell me your father's name.'

For in those times, mothers devoured men like she-wolves and insulted them until the last breath they drew.

CHAPTER 73

The Castle of Grief

In the past, Christians called mortuary chapels *castra doloris* because they were castle-shaped structures closed off by railings.

°The funeral service for Louis de Bourbon, Prince of Condé was celebrated on 10 March 1686 at Notre-Dame in Paris.

Madame de Sévigné wrote that the ceremony that took place on this occasion was 'the most triumphant funeral ever held since mortals have existed'. Jean Berain the Elder made drawings of the event. He had them engraved. They were put on sale as prints. Berain himself appended to them the title *Camp de la Douleur* (*castrum doloris*) in red ink. The cortège was led by a line of one hundred poor folk. Each had been given a coat of grey cloth, a pair of shoes, a white three-franc piece. Staggering from hunger, but driven on by the promise of food and wine, they processed with white wax torches in their hands.

As they entered the city's cathedral church, the onlookers were moved. It was thought that the hundred poor folk were reeling from pain, whereas they were famished and thinking only of the meal they had been promised. The royal guests gathered there wept at the sight.

*

The *castrum doloris* is melancholia.

In mourning, the one you loved is dead and you see their face, their heart-breaking photograph, catch a glimpse of them walking in the street (though it cannot be them), see their ghost in dreams.

In melancholia you see nothing. Everything becomes unknown and the cause of every pain, of every sadness is unknown. Time is unknown. Memories are unknown. The world is unknown. You are back at the helpless distress of your earliest moments, when you first came into the light. *Newness.* Loss, reality, name, mourning—even *nihil* is lacking.

CHAPTER 74

Post-mortem Assaults on Reputation

In the Western world in the late eighties, post-mortem assaults on reputation suddenly made their appearance.

°Bruno Bettelheim had written the two finest books ever devoted to mutilation and autism. The announcement of his suicide was met with *a carnival of hatred*. I remember it with a vivid sense of disgust. The collective morality, both American and European, refused to accept that a doctor of psychoanalysis, who was responsible for treating others, should put his head in a plastic bag, kneel down by his front door, collapse head first on to the doormat and undermine optimism. In France, the loathing expressed took on an antisemitic character. It would have been better, they said, if he had been a timber merchant in Vienna and an anonymous deportee to the camps. In the United States, they wrote: Why did this hideous refugee from the death camps come and commit suicide in our country? Was that any way to show gratitude to his hosts?

This was in spring 1990.

The 'burial truce' was a thing of the past.

This was the first time I discovered that, in societies obsessed with egalitarian competition, fervid denigration could be inflicted posthumously on the dead themselves.

The automatic courtesy of not speaking ill of the dead was discarded.

I experienced this terrible passion once again the day after Marguerite Duras died. I was sad that that tiny body had expired. I used to love to see her push open the door of the little office I occupied at the time in a publisher's behind the St Thomas Aquinas church in Paris' seventh arrondissement.

I read the newspapers. I watched the television. I read the weeklies. The world they revealed frightened me. People long ago gave up on the inviolability of the home, freedom of expression, private life, sexual difference, paternal authority, and the privacy of telephone communications. Now they were giving up on respect for corpses within an hour of their falling silent. This was civil war extended to the dead. The war of all against each had begun and there were no longer any rights that might stand in its way. This was the 'live' lynching of corpses.

*

°Father Coton told a suddenly troubled King Henri IV: 'Jesus will deliver the Last Judgement in Syriac.'

*

When he preached his Lenten sermons at the Louvre, Father Pierre Coton provided these precise details on hell: Hell is a charnel house into which the angels throw all the refuse of human bodies, from the first murderer and fratricide to the Antichrist and his followers. Hell is an accumulation of such great tortures that, beside it, all other punishments in the past, present or future—scorpions, racks, wheels, breastplates, grills, brazen bulls, helms of fire, millstones, flayings, dislocations, cuttings, impalings, piercings, convulsions, distressings and contractions of nerves—are mere dew upon the grass.

CHAPTER 75

The Cat

A drop of ink connects in some little way with the night that preceded the source of each body. Reading, writing, living: magnetic fields into which are thrown the iron filings of adventures, sorrows, chance events, episodes, fragments, wounds. I consigned the fruits of my reading to a whole library of little black and red binders. These binders followed me round for forty years in the valley of the Seine and the valley of the Yonne. I no longer knew whether I was writing with them or for them. One day Isaac Bashevis Singer was asked why he persisted in writing his books in Yiddish when all his readers had been exterminated in the death camps.

'For their shades,' he replied.

One writes better for the eyes of those one loved than with the intention of submitting oneself to the gaze of those who will dominate one.

One writes for lost eyes. One can love the dead. I loved the dead. I did not like the death in the dead. I liked the fear they had felt for it.

Death is the *ultima linea* on which the letters of language are written, the notes of music inscribed.

The narration made possible by half-bleached words cut out from the written language hurls men into ghostliness.

Misfortune calls forth from us dead eyes to diminish it.

From animals to men a glance is enough to understand.

A true book is this sure glance.

*

I felt a slight itch in the middle of my palm. That was what a ghost was. A missing caress. I already had in my hand the desire to stroke an animal that was soft and warm and whose spine would suddenly arch beneath my fingers, while a low sound panted, purred, swelled and evened, ending in a continuous low buzz like the bourdon stop of the organ.

In the shoes in the bottom of the cupboard, which the cat liked to retreat to when he wasn't happy, was where he wanted to die.

He had slipped under the spare cot, on top of the folded deckchair, by the wooden box with the hammer, nails and picture hooks and the bulbs you screw into lamp sockets.

CHAPTER 76

The lawn was neglected. Moss had invaded it on the eastern side over some 65 feet. The ground was bare now as far as the garage wall. In the south there was clover. The grass was struggling to make room for itself between the trees, bushes, daisies, mosses and mud.

There was even bracken.

There were lots of duck droppings which he had carefully to avoid unless he had taken the trouble to slip his feet into rubber boots. He was weary. He was a little anaemic. He wasn't even capable of holding a spade for long. He managed to stick it in the ground, could even tip it back, but lifting it filled his mouth with fresh blood. His lips suddenly became as red as felspar in the forests of the Ardennes or an ancient gemstone lying in deep water. He wasn't a man, he was a clown. He took his handkerchief. He wiped his red lips and nose. He went to rest on the bank and sat down on the cold wall above the black boats. He watched the water endlessly flowing by. The cold penetrated the material of his trousers and gradually seeped into his loins. So he went in. He made a fire. He read. One day, while reading and coughing a little, he died. When he arrived among the dead, he came by chance on Ariosto whom he knew well and he was delighted to see him again. He took him by the arm. He said to him, 'And where's Tasso?' Ariosto took him to Tasso. He took him by the hand. He pressed his hand. He said, 'I'd like to see Armida.' Tasso took him first to Giambattista Lulli who eventually took him to Armida. But she turned away as soon as she saw him. Then she spun sharply round and beckoned him to follow. He followed her. She walked quickly. Armida suddenly stumbled over a corpse. Immediately, she mutilated it. She decked out the corpse in the arms of Rinaldo. That way she was able to make people believe he had died. That done, she went back down to the shore of the Oronto. There was a narrow, red boat there, gently bumping against the bank with each surge of the water. She told him: 'Now you'll understand that I have to forget this dead man I've cut up.'

There were a dozen flowers, scattered among the grass, each finer and more colourful than the last. She crossed the meadow. She went down to the water. She knelt. She leant over. She examined her reflection. She dreamt. She repeated pointlessly to herself:

'I have to forget this dead man with whom I was in love. The face reflected in the passing current at this moment is that of a woman. But what is finer than the body of a living man at the moment when he desires her?'

In truth, godesses love lands more than adventures, adventures more than love affairs, love affairs more than men.

CHAPTER 77

Porte Saint-Ouen

At the Porte Saint-Ouen market, in a cardboard box, he found a photograph. He picked it up and viewed it with amazement. In the bathroom with the two glazed walls, covered in art nouveau tiles, adjacent to the second-floor bedroom in the house at Ancenis, standing in front of the black-laquered chest of drawers with the grey mirror on top of it, a young woman was looking at herself. °It was my great-great-great-aunt on the arm of Maurice Rollinat. What was written on the back of the photograph, the attribution—everything was right about it. In my house on the river Yonne at Sens, I kept a copy of the marriage certificate. I handed over a little grey five-euro note.

I put the photograph back on the mantelpiece, slipping it into the edge of the plaster cornice of the old mirror.

Dark mirrors.

Window panes in the night time are dark mirrors.

We don't have much of a shadow ourselves when evening falls.

I went to the drawer that I'd come to look in and pulled it right out. I sat down and placed it on my knees. I read the letters. Everything gets stolen. Everything gets sold.

You don't know where your life is hidden.

°Mozart had put his life into a little canary that Marianne looked after in Salzburg and fed to the end.

Pushkin had put his life into a parrot.

Bidasari into a goldfish.

In our case, it was a concealed house, a mirror hanging by a rusty iron chain. The mirror was leaning over a Godin stove. Then the reflections had gone from the mirror; the soul had gone from its lips.

CHAPTER 78

Old Thunderstorm

In 1838 Emily wrote in her notebook: 'Bronte in Greek means thunder.'

In 888 in Japan, the daughter of the governor of the province of Ise was appointed lady-in-waiting to the Empress Onshi.

*

Little by little, the daughter of the governor of the province of Ise became a close friend of the empress. When she had reached the age of seventeen, she fell in love with Prince Nakahira. That love was reciprocated and it was so impossible to conceal that it was immediately known to everyone.

Whenever these two faces saw one another, they beamed.

One winter's day, standing by a brazier, she hid her face behind her hands and told him: 'I love you.'

On the first day of spring, she told the prince: 'I can feel your sex in me like a torrent.'

On the first day of summer, she told him: 'I feel that the depths of my heart are much darker than the foliage spreading all round us.'

Prince Nakahira had agreed to be joined in marriage to a more powerful family than that of the governor of the province of Ise. He therefore went to find the daughter of the governor of the province of Ise. He broke with her.

Though he had become the husband of another, with six months gone his love for the daughter of the governor of the province of Ise still endured in his heart. He wanted to approach her again. He wrote to her. He told her he would at least like to be able to show her his affection for, naturally, he would not be so bold as to indicate his desire.

She did not reply to his letter.

He sent a relative.

She felt compelled to receive him but melancholy filled the young woman's heart. She replied: 'I cannot do as the prince asks. It is certainly not that my love has diminished. It is that I no longer wish to. It is certainly not because I have suffered a great deal and have been disappointed in love. It is because I have, over time, drowned myself in waiting, as the branches of the trees drown in fog in the days of autumn. Do you think you are capable of reporting these words to Prince Nakahira?'

'No.'

Then she agreed that he should write down her feelings as she dictated them to him. She began.

'I have drowned.'

'The prince will not understand. He will think you have drowned.'

'Are men not, then, as intelligent as they claim?'

'Possibly not.'

'Simply tell him that I cannot leave sadness behind, as though I were merely leaving a room.'

'The prince will not understand. I think what you are saying is an image.'

'Then write: "Prince, it is not possible for me to meet you as though now were a day in times gone by."'

The message was written down as she dictated but the messenger did not write well enough, since he did not understand what he was writing.

She took the brush and the letter from his hands. She tore up the letter. She said to the messenger:

'We are not, in the end, going to write. You will say precisely to your master: "You left me and you will not see me again. I am no longer the girl you once fell in love with. Nor am I any longer the young woman you abandoned to the loneliness of summer. I am now nothing but a misty, insubstantial figure. I have gradually faded in this mist." Please repeat what I have said.'

The messenger repeated the message until he knew it by heart and off he went.

*

At first, Prince Nakahira was frightened by the distress he had caused in choosing an other than the daughter of the governor of the province of Ise as his wife. But with the passage of time he nevertheless pressed his attentions upon his former mistress. He sent a cart full of musicians to her. It was the prince's former nurse who led the company. The daughter of the governor of the province of Ise was moved to see her again. She embraced her as though she had been her mother but listen she would not. The musicians tuned their instruments and launched into their songs but she would have none of it.

'Please tell the prince he is to respect his good lady wife and keep the oath he made when he married her.'

She left them. Next day the nurse returned; she was in tears; she pressed the prince's case further; she described his distraught state; she pointed out that his regret was sincere; she showed how greatly his mind was troubled by remorse; how strong his love still was.

'Madam, you are like my mother and I respect you as such.'

'Remember that I am also like a mother to the prince and this is why I keep on pressing his case. On certain matters I can exert an influence on his mind.'

'But, do you see, I never knew my mother. I am a woman who killed her mother when I was born.'

'The prince knows all that. He has told me that ten times over. Why do you think he sent me to persuade you?'

'Then I shall ask you to take down a letter from me. Will you do so?'

The former nurse to the prince sat down and took up a brush. The daughter of the governor of the province of Ise then dictated this letter:

'Prince, never say farewell to those around you. That word has powers over the ears that hear it. I am well placed to know that the words you use represent nothing for yourself but not everyone is like you. I lost my way prematurely on the road that leads to the mountain of the dead, remembering the words you pronounced in former times. Mist, cotton wool, clouds, steam—that is the world I am approaching. Be aware that what you promised the one you loved was even more insubstantial.'

But Prince Nakahira dreamt of her. She too was constantly visited by his image in her dreams. Eventually they saw one another again. She truly made an effort to love him again. On several occasions they withdrew again into the night. But despite all her efforts—despite perfuming herself and praying to the gods, despite much dreaming, dressing herself with greater attentiveness and drinking one or two cups of piping-hot rice wine—she could no longer abandon herself to him as once she had, so greatly had her soul been wounded.

Similarly, the prince could no longer find the paths to her consent or her elation. He was afraid of the pain he made her feel once more by undressing and embracing her. He could tell it was not joy he immediately triggered in her. The sighs she heaved had about them something of a lament.

Soon, he no longer even had the virile potency to enter her in the night as she slept.

He was so moved by the suffering he had caused in the past by ceasing to be faithful to her that he lost his own capacities as a result.

One dawn, he told her:

'When you are at my side I can no longer raise my eyes towards you as I did in the past.'

'It isn't only your eyes you can't raise when you see me,' she told the prince. 'I realized that your desire was failing when you were in my arms.'

'That is what I meant.'

'Then be more frank. Say, I can't get an erection. Don't remain a constant stranger to the truth. Stop your endless deceiving of me.'

'I have to admit I no longer desire you as I once did. I cannot explain it.'

Then she replied: 'This comes at just the right moment, since you have a wife who awaits the weight of your body being placed upon her, so that it may reproduce itself twice more. I have seen this in a dream.'

'The dream you have had is no sure oracle. It so happens that my wife's flesh attracts me even less than your sadness.'

'I think that if sadness is the shore on which I stand, an interminable languour will be yours and you have little to gain from it. Sadness and languour now face one another all along the unfordable river.'

'They say that only the first love can help the dead man's soul to cross hell's river. You are my first love.'

'That is no doubt true but for me you are the only one.'

'So?'

'So the gods do not say that love, whether the first love or the only love, carries you across the river of the dead with erections and orgasms.'

'Drought, cold and darkness have risen up from hell,' murmured the prince.

'One day you forced me to choose between waiting and distaste and you plunged me into an impalpable mist.'

'The drought was for you and the coldness for me.'

'The waiting for you and the distaste for me.'

This is what the daughter of the governor of the province of Ise replied to Prince Nakahira. They did not see one another again for nine years.

*

They saw one another for the last day of the tenth spring that fell to them in the story of their love. But the joy had gone from their meetings, at the same time as the sensual delight had left them. She did not speak a word to him.

They merely bowed to one another, weeping.

Later he sent her letters to which she did not reply.

She simply noted 'Seen' on the missives he sent her, to indicate that she had taken cognizance of them. After writing 'Seen', she returned them to him. But never again did she deign to impart her impressions regarding the thoughts he confided to her.

She was a lover who repeated that she had not been disappointed by love but by her lover.

He wrote to her: 'At least, let me see you in silence. I shall place my cheek on your breast. I shall smell your fragrance. I shall weep against your soft skin, though I am no longer able to give you pleasure.'

But she no longer wished to hear speak either of nudity or perfumes or embraces.

*

Years later, at the New Year celebrations, he once again sent one of his relatives to take her a packet of salt, on the paper wrapping of which he had written this quatrain:

'Sea spray.

Endless swell.

I am thinking of you.

I am drowning.'

She could not help but laugh at such grandiloquence.

She said to this relative: 'Tell him that on the seashore the shells that were broken have become sand.'

In the spring of 904 he swore an oath that he would send his wife away. And that is what he did. He repudiated his wife. He offered the daughter of the governor of the province of Ise a palace on a southern island. But she told the two horsemen who had come bearing his message: 'Let him make no gifts, because he takes them back. And let him add no oaths, since he breaks them.'

*

The bonds between them slackened. Age overtook their bodies, as darkness overtakes evening. He continued, nevertheless, to write her a letter each autumn.

They did not see one another again.

All fragments of poems, of diaries and even of drafts of letters of the Empress Onshi's companion have been conserved. Including this quatrain:

'The old bridge of Nagara
In the bay of Osaka,
By waves coming from out at sea,
Is destroyed each year.'

And also this lament, which the daughter of the governor of the province of Ise had written when she learnt that Prince Nakahira had, immediately after repudiating his wife, taken very young concubines:

'Over the old bridge of Nagara
No one passes any more.

Beneath the bridge
No boat sinks.'

She took flight suddenly to a deserted spot, withhold-
ing her whereabouts from the prince. However, he
had his people spy on her. He discovered her hiding
place but did not have the strength to go to her again.
She learnt that he had withdrawn from the court following a plot. All his friends disappeared. Once again
he sent a wagon for her. She, however, sent it back,
dictating to his relative these words to be reported to
the prince: 'Thank you, Prince, but no. I cannot take
you in my arms, for I am now merely a thunderstorm.
An old thunderstorm.'

CHAPTER 79

Quomodo dicis quod amas me

Quomodo dicis quod amas me? How can you say you love me? This is what Delilah says to Samson before sending him to his death, when she has wrung from him the secret of his strength.

Lovers at the end of their love choose either an ambassador among the living or an emissary among the dead.

The ambassador among the living is a child, by which every woman prolongs the shadow of the man or of his force within her. Then the child assumes all the active space the man's potency was supposed to occupy. Once the woman has been impregnated, the man who helped in the conception is abandoned at the door of the world of mothers.

The emissary among the dead is suicide, in which the future deceased is eager to return as a ghost. This means endless guilt, vengeance and pain, poisoning forever the world he or she leaves behind.

Child or death—there is in either case a shadow.

*

A potter's daughter called Dibutades lived at Corinth where she loved a young man who was extremely handsome. He had to go off to war. On their last night together she didn't clasp him to her. She didn't even kiss him. She raised up an oil lamp in her left hand. She took in her right a piece of charcoal from the brazier. She went up to him. She did not caress the volume of his body which was, nonetheless, all her desire. Using the piece of charcoal, she chose instead to outline his shadow on the surface of the wall behind him.

*

There was in France, in days gone by, a strange custom known as the *danse du regret*. On the day of a wedding, the suitor who had been supplanted by a rival was forced to dance with the bride before the assembled company.

As a preliminary, a carpet was unrolled on the floor of the room and this was then covered with a blanket to muffle the sound of their steps entirely.

After the bride had danced noiselessly with the ousted suitor in front of everyone, including her husband in his wedding clothes, she no longer had the right to see him.

The 'silence' extinguished the coitus which the 'dance' represented as though in a dream.

*

Max Brod tells how Kafka, coming home one afternoon, startled his father, who was dozing on the living-room sofa. Franz Kafka gestured to his father with an upraised arm and, tiptoeing across the room, whispered:

'Don't wake up, Papa. Treat me like a dream.'

CHAPTER 80

Oxford means, literally, 'ford of the oxen'.

At the hotel I had to give a false name at the desk. The absolutely crucial difficulty in my life was not to forget the alias I was using when I had to give the hotelier my name. I said to myself: 'I'm the battle between the ford and the mysterious ferryman. She is woman feigning death.'

'But she's alive.'

'Yes.'

'So why say she isn't?'

'I'm ashamed of having passed her off as dead.'

'And are you going to tell her I'm dead?'

'Yes, but that isn't a lie. You *are* dead.'

The plane is coming in over Naples. I wake suddenly. I was dreaming of Cäcilia Müller. I thought I was coming in to Barcelona. I got off the plane. I climbed the stairs. Cäcilia opened the door.

She is eighteen years old.

'How old you are!' are the words with which she greets me.

She kisses me. She is not married. She is very beautiful. We eat. We eat a lot. There are lots of people around us. I tell her that I fell asleep on the plane and dreamt of her.

'That's normal. It's because you were coming to see me,' she remarks.

Someone rings the doorbell. It's a very long ring, very strident.

'That's odd,' says Cilly, 'I'm not expecting anyone. I'll go see who it is. Don't worry. Have some more to eat.'

She comes running back in a panic.

'It's your mother!'

I go to the door. Mum is waiting for me on the landing. She doesn't seem happy. She is wearing a raincoat with a little fur hat on her head. She says: 'I've been waiting for you for hours to go out.'

I rush to put my coat on. I am knotting my scarf. But my mother has run off at full tilt down the street because she has seen a cat and is terrified. She is running too fast. Shouting too loudly. I give up on the idea of following her. I crouch down. I take the cat's face in my hands. I press my forehead against its forehead.

'Oh, my friend!'

He puts his paw on my hand.

'Oh, my velvet paw!'

Over a thirty-year career, François Pontrain, a grave digger at the cemetery of the Innocents in Paris, buried 90,107 bodies. He kept a sorrowful reckoning of his work, recording each name in his register with a quill pen, as well as taking each body in his arms to bury it, before covering it with earth. Some people lead gloomy lives. François Pontrain had a spade, a little square of earth, a pot of ink, a pen, a knife and a yellow register. He himself died in 1572, borne off in the arms of some unknown individual, with no one's pen to record his passing.

CHAPTER 83

Lille

I got to Lille late in the day. It was Thursday, 10 October 2002. I walked out of the station. The sky was blue. It was a fine day. I walked up the avenue and pushed open the door of the church of Saint-Maurice. I entered its silence and half light. I looked at the great black, bituminous, impenetrable canvases. I sat down.

In front of me a young woman in a blue nylon apron was blowing out the candles on the altars.

When she got to the chapels, she blew out the red oil lamps.

In a side chapel near the entrance a group of women of all ages were reciting the rosary by turns, then singing it quietly to themselves.

Suddenly, a group of young people came in noisily, hurling abuse at the god of the Catholics. The youngsters ran screaming right into the choir. They had come in through the door leading to the Lille-Flandres station. They were bounding around and laughing. They mentioned the name of a Muslim hero of the Middle East.

The litanies to the Virgin fell silent. The ageing singers huddled together.

The shattering cries combined, filling the nave with sound. They grew even louder. The youngsters were testing the acoustics. There were five of them, very young, with their schoolbags on their shoulders or their backs.

An old priest in trousers pushed open a glass door, behind which he was hearing confession. He advanced unsteadily across the flagstones in rubber shoes lined with white wool. He went over and quietly parleyed with them for a brief moment. He had no difficulty seeing them out of the building, these young boys whose voices had already broken. They left in silence but not without pride. They were like the Vikings sailing up the Seine and Yonne rivers on their way to attack Paris and Vézelay. The old priest in the squeaky rubber shoes snuffed out the last candles. He gestured to me to get up. He closed up the church behind me. I walked on. I went up towards the city. I no longer belonged to any particular world. I no longer had anything to lean on. I wandered the dark streets of Lille where they were waiting for me in a bookshop on the rue Esquermoise. The price of freedom is the total vulnerability to which it abandons you. If we no longer depend on anyone's power, we can no longer expect help from any quarter. The churches had become the only reservoirs of emptiness, depth, silence and abyssality for the few atheists who still existed in this world.

CHAPTER 84

The Bay of Naples in 1552

The Bay of Naples was at that time a group of forts built upon ruins. Naples was a village. A few fishermen were casting their nets. Some peasants were digging over the fields of tuff.

The scene takes place in 1552.

°One by one, Brantôme refers by name to the skiffs and galleys on station in the cove and the vessel arriving: he is still sailing the Tyrrhenian sea.

On the quayside three soldiers dressed in crimson velvet are waiting.

Brantôme and the captain go down the gangway.

Brantôme and the captain get into a coach harnessed to black chargers.

CHAPTER 85

Seven fishermen living in Herculaneum were suffocated by gases in the boatshed adjoining the beach.

In 1661 Pu Songling wrote that the man of letters is the one who records the numbers of the drowned. On the one side, the list of the empty boats. On the other, the list of human beings missing from their benches. The lake is Dongting. The man of letters is Liu Yi.

Each time he showed an object, that object was unknown. He was like a finder of hidden things that have no name and no identifiable shape.

Along the bank in the port of Givet there was a long string of six battered, old barges before you got to the post office.

In Vienna, Freud's apartment is empty. The doctor's plaque remains, together with the coat peg (a scarf, an umbrella). The waiting room is empty. All the other rooms are bare. The National Socialist Party has gone by. Beneath Freud's empty apartment there is a seller of boats and small craft.

Exhibited in the window of 19 Berggasse on 16 November 2003 was a large white dinghy, a dark-green three-seater plastic canoe, a pedalo and, at the back of the shop, a handsome wooden barge painted blue.

CHAPTER 86

Charon's Bark

But it wasn't a bark, it was a hydrofoil. We climbed on to the iron gangway. We took the hydrofoil, the *aliscafo*, and left the island. The boat was moving so much and she was so frightened that I took her tiny hand in mine. There was something of a swell. There were many waves. It was the beginning of autumn. We disembarked. We climbed the side of the hill. In the pale sun, the Parco di Virgilio was very beautiful and shrouded in mist. The lawn was empty and blue. The silence was total. There seemed to be no one there. The child did not speak. I lost sight of her. I found her again at the corner of the warden's house. She was crouching by the big bed of white fritillaries. She was four years old. She was picking up the dead leaves, smoothing them out, unfolding them at some length on her thigh with the palm of her hand and arranging them, piling them in her glossy blue plastic bag that sparkled in the sun. We waited a long time at the bus stop. The road leading up to Vesuvius by the western side ran in long loops over Monte Eremo. A kilometre from Colle Umberto, we reached the car park and got off the bus. We did up the laces of our big walking boots. She rubbed at the tips of her fingers because they were covered in ash. We walked down the little lava path that leads to the Valle dell'Inferno. Then we came back by the cliff path. The wind from the sea suddenly hit us as we reached the cliff top. The air above it was an enormous transparent wave that reached into the sky and suddenly surged back towards us. The blue of the sky tinged the people's clothing, the clothing of all of us who were leaning forward, looking down at the shore below, the sea below and the boat coming silently towards the island; leaning over the wall of tuff that had crumbled on to the black strand. A scene of extraordinary beauty.

TRANSLATOR'S NOTES

Chapter 1

° *In 1690 Furetière spelt it* corbillard . . . The reference is to French writer Antoine Furetière (1619–88), whose dictionary was posthumously published in two volumes in Rotterdam in 1690.

Chapter 3

° *In the past the horse-drawn* gabarres . . . The *gabarre* (from Occitan *gabarra*) is a traditional vessel used to transport goods.

Chapter 4

° *In those days Stéphane* . . . Mallarmé (1842–98) found fame as a poet under the name Stéphane, a variant of his birth name Étienne. His sister Maria died in 1857.

Chapter 6

° *Salomon of London* . . . The German-born violinist and impresario Johann Peter Salomon (1745–1815) moved to London in the early 1780s.

Chapter 7

° *All the little Perret buildings* . . . The neoclassical architect Auguste Perret was instrumental in the reconstruction of the centre of Le Havre between 1945 and 1954. His work was denigrated at the time by Modernists such as Le Corbusier, but the reconstructed area is now listed as a UNESCO World Heritage Site.

° *One day, a hunter* . . . The Grotte Carriot near Cahors, Lot, France, was named after Robert Carriot who discovered its wall paintings in 1969.

° *I can still see the insubstantial, white coins* . . . The May 1958 crisis was a political crisis in France during the Algerian War of Independence (1954–62). It led to Charles de Gaulle returning to power after a ten-year absence.

Chapter 10

° *'What is hell?' asked Massillon* . . . Jean-Baptiste Massillon (1663–1742) was a celebrated French preacher. He was bishop of Clermont from 1717 until his death.

Chapter 11

° *These are the words Cardinal Mazarin used* . . . Jules Mazarin (1602–61) was first minister of France from 1642 to 1661.

○ *He himself told Lionne on 1 November 1659 . . .* Hugues de Lionne (1611–71) was a prominent French diplomat and statesman.

Chapter 13

○ *Madame de Sévigné took up her pen again . . .* Marie de Rabutin-Chantal, marquise de Sévigné (1626–96) was a French noble-woman whose letters convey a lively portrait of French aristocratic life in the seventeenth century. Madame de La Fayette (Marie-Madeleine Pioche de La Vergne, comtesse de La Fayette, 1634–93) was the author of *La Princesse de Clèves*, France's first historical novel.

Chapter 14

○ *The last tournament to take place in Normandy . . .* Arques-la-Bataille in Upper Normandy boasts an eleventh-century castle built by William of Talou.

Chapter 16

○ *Queen Marie Leszczyńska had asked . . .* Queen Marie Leszczyńska was the wife of Louis XV.

Chapter 17

○ *Maubert is a contraction of Maître Albert . . .* The name Maubert is familiar to Parisians from the Place Maubert or the Maubert-Mutualité metro station.

Chapter 18

° *Homer says of him in the* Iliad . . . This passage from Homer is taken from William Cowper's verse translation of the *Iliad*.

Chapter 22

° *Every reader is like Saint Alexis* . . . Saint Alexis or Alexius is said to have lived for seventeen years under the stairs in the home of his parents, unrecognized by them, after seventeen years spent as a pious Christian beggar in Syria.

° *Melanie Klein*: *'To feel alone is the programme.'* . . . Pascal Quignard renders this same phrase in two different ways in the French (see chapter 31) and I have followed his usage in the translation without attempting to restore the original English.

° *He would be setting out on an adventure* . . . The reference here is to *l'ancienne matière de Bretagne*, the ancient 'matter of Brittany', a fund of stories possibly taken from the repertory of Celtic storytellers or from manuscript sources no longer extant, which feed into the poetry of the twelfth and thirteenth centuries—most notably the writings of Chrétien de Troyes and Marie de France.

° *'S'il vous plaît nous laissez écrire* . . . These lines were originally penned by Clément Marot (1496–1544).

Chapter 27

° *'But of that day . . . knoweth no man'* . . . in Mark 13:32.

Chapter 29

○ *Navarrus wrote:* ... Navarrus (1491–1584), whose real name was Martin de Azpilcueta, was a leading Spanish theologian and professor of canon law.

○ *One day Peter said to Jesus* ... in Mark 9:5.

Chapter 33

○ *It is the* secessio plebis ... Withdrawal of the commoners or secession of the plebs.

○ *It was* Der Weg ins Freie ... Literally: the way (or path) into the open. A 1923 English translation by Horace Samuel has been published both as *The Road to the Open* and *The Road into the Open*.

Chapter 36

○ *Étienne de La Boétie wrote* ... La Boétie (1530–63) was a writer, judge and friend of the great essayist and philosopher Montaigne. He himself made a major contribution to sixteenth-century political philosophy.

○ *At the end of the Second World War* ... 'No one' here is in English in the original.

Chapter 41

○ *Bossuet's Mouth* ... Jacques-Bénigne Bossuet (1627–1704) was a French theologian and bishop. He was court preacher to

Louis XIV and is renowned for his sermons and funeral orations, including that for Henrietta Anne of England, daughter of Charles I, known as Henriette d'Angleterre.

Chapter 44

° *In his* Towards Myself, *Marcus Aurelius . . .* The text by Marcus Aurelius is known in English as *The Meditations*. Quignard uses his own translation of the title here, *Vers moi-même*, the standard French translations being *Pensées à moi-même* and *Pensées pour moi-même*. The passage in question is from Book 9, Section 3.

Chapter 45

° *In the* Nekuomanteia, *Lucian writes . . .* Quignard refers to this text as '*la Nèkyomancie*'. In English, it is commonly called *Menippus or Oracle of the Dead*.

Chapter 47

° *He threw his body into the waters of the Seine that flow towards the port of Le Havre de Grâce . . .* This is the modern city of Le Havre.

Chapter 50

° *The* virtus *of a* fascinus *. . . Fascinus* is the Roman term for what we commonly term the phallus.

Chapter 51

° *then Servius Tullius was born* . . . Servius Tullius was the sixth king of ancient Rome.

°` *In a painting by Georges de La Tour* . . . The picture is probably *Saint Joseph the Carpenter*, oil on canvas (1640s), currently in the Louvre.

Chapter 54

° Phusis *has its forerunner in* rhusis . . . *Rhusis* means a flowing or flow.

Chapter 55

° *Franz Süssmayr: 'I complete the masterpieces* . . . Franz Xaver Süssmayr (born in Schwanenstadt in 1766, died in Vienna in 1803) is famous for completing Mozart's *Requiem*.

Chapter 57

° *Franz Kafka wrote to Oskar Pollak in 1904* . . . This is from a letter of 27 January 1904. See Franz Kafka, *Letters to Friends, Family and Editors* (Richard and Clara Winston trans) (London: Oneworld Classics Ltd., 2011), p. 16.

Chapter 58

° *Behold, Lord, we have forsaken all.* . . . Matthew 19:27: 'Behold, we have forsaken all, and followed thee: what shall we have therefore?' (King James Bible).

Chapter 59

° *It was the day the Lion of Belfort was erected* . . . The Lion of Belfort is a monumental sculpture symbolizing the resistance of the French to the Prussian siege of that city in 1870–71. It was sculpted by Frédéric Bartholdi, creator of New York's Statue of Liberty.

Chapter 65

° *Gabriel Le Bras said*: '*The sociology of irreligion is the most moving chapter in the history of groups.*' . . . Gabriel Le Bras (1891–1970) was a pioneering sociologist of religion and a professor of canon law at Strasbourg and Paris.

° De arte nihil credendi *was written in late adolescence, as was* La Boétie's Contr'un . . . La Boétie's *Contr'un* bears the alternative title *Discours de la servitude volontaire* (Discourse on Voluntary Servitude).

Chapter 66

° *It was Gentillet who, in the late sixteenth century, stated that being an atheist was synonymous with being 'literary'* . . . Innocent Gentillet (1535–88), the Huguenot author of the *Anti-Machiavel*, was a French lawyer and theologian.

° *They leant over and murmured*: 'De tribus impostoribus!' . . . *The Treatise of the Three Impostors* (De Tribus Impostoribus) is the name for a probable mythical work supposedly denying all three Abrahamic religions—Judaism, Christianity and Islam.

° *Pirithous the Atheist said*: 'Ficta. *They are fables. The gods are without power.*' . . . These lines are from Book 8 of Ovid's *Metamorphoses.*

° *He turned to the eldest of Benjamin Franklin's grandchildren who was called Temple* . . . William Temple Franklin (born in London in 1760 and died in Paris in 1823), known as Temple, was an American diplomat, secretary to the American delegation that negotiated US independence at the Treaty of Paris in 1783.

Chapter 67

° *Jesus said to them*: '*There is none.*' . . . '*Christus*! ist kein Gott?' Er antwortete: 'Es ist keiner.'

° '*We are orphans. You, I, we are orphans. There is no father.*' . . . '*Wir sind alle Waisen, ich und ihr, wir sind ohne Vater.*'

° *The second 'God is dead' scene* . . . Edgar Quinet's dramatic prose poem *Ahasvérus* was first published in Paris in 1833.

° 'Ich hab'mein Sac' auf Nichts gestellt.' '*I have taken nothingness as my cause.*' . . . I have stayed very close to Quignard's translation of Stirner here. Stirner's English translator Steven T. Byington preferred to translate this line from Goethe's poem '*Vanitas Vanitatum Vanitas*' as 'All things are nothing to me', while adding a literal translation: 'I have set my affair on nothing.' See Max Stirner, *The Ego and his Own* (New York: Benjamin R. Tucker, 1907), p. 9.

° *Hegel wrote in the* Phenomenology of Spirit *of Luther's 'hard saying that "God is dead".* . . . See *Phenomenology of Spirit* (A. V. Miller trans.) (Oxford: Oxford University Press, 1977), p. 455.

Chapter 68

° *When she appeared before the Fourth War Council, Louise Michel* . . . Louise Michel (1830–1905) was a French anarchist revolutionary and one of the most prominent figures of the Paris Commune, for her part in which she was deported to New Caledonia in 1873.

Chapter 69

° *Those men are termed superstitious* (superstitiosi) . . . *'Qui totos dies precabantur et immolabant, ut sibi sui liberi superstites essent, superstitiosi sunt appellati.'* Those who prayed and offered sacrifice for whole days that their children might survive them, were called superstitious (Cicero, *De natura deorum*, 2.28.72).

° *Saint-Evremond said the world of the living was merely another hell situated between earth and moon* . . . Charles de Saint-Evremond (1613–1703) was a French essayist and literary critic. He died in exile in London and is buried in Poet's Corner.

Chapter 70

° *That there are somewhere Manes* . . . In Roman religion, the Manes were the deified souls of the departed.

° *This is what Juvenal said in* Satires II, *149* . . . Juvenal: '*Esse aliquos manes et subterranea regna et contum et Stygio ranas in gurgite nigras, atque una transire vadum tot milia cumba nec pueri credunt . . .*'

Chapter 71

° *Henrietta Anne of England, who was at Saint-Cloud* . . . Henrietta Anne (1644–70) was the daughter of Charles I and of Queen Henrietta Maria of France.

° *Never mind the marvellous words spoken by Bossuet* . . . One of the most famous of Bossuet's celebrated funeral orations was that delivered upon the death of Henrietta Anne of England.

Chapter 72

° *Image of pride:* Imago feritatis . . . '*Image de la fierté:* Imago *feritatis.*' *Feritas* in Latin means wildness, fierceness, savageness, roughness.

Chapter 73

° *The funeral service for Louis de Bourbon, Prince of Condé* . . . Louis de Bourbon, Prince of Condé (1621–86), Duke of Enghien until his father's death in 1646 and later known, for his military prowess, as 'Le Grand Condé', was one of the leading generals of the age.

Chapter 74

° *Bruno Bettelheim had written the two finest books ever devoted to mutilation and autism* . . . The Austrian-born psychologist Bruno Bettelheim (1903–90) became a naturalized American in 1944. The books referred to are probably *Symbolic Wounds* (1956) and *The Empty Fortress* (1967).

° *Father Coton told a suddenly troubled king Henri IV:* 'Jesus will deliver the Last Judgement in Syriac.' . . . Le Père Coton (1564–1626) was a French Jesuit priest, a renowned preacher and writer and the confessor of Kings Henri IV and Louis XIII.

Chapter 77

° *It was my great-great-great-aunt on the arm of Maurice Rollinat* . . . Maurice Rollinat (1846–1903) was a French poet who enjoyed some success in the late nineteenth century. He was a member of the literary circle 'Les Hydropathes', founded by Émile Goudeau.

° *Mozart had put his life into a little canary that Marianne looked after* . . . Maria Anna Thekla Mozart, known as Marianne, was Mozart's cousin, with whom he exchanged a lively correspondence.

Chapter 84

° *One by one, Brantôme refers by name* . . . Brantôme (1540–1614) was a French soldier, adventurer and memoirist.